AN EXPECTATION OF PLENTY

AN EXPECTATION OF PLENTY

Thomas Bazar

Hello Melissa,

Enjoy The book!

T.B. 10/10/20

atmosphere press

*To my father, thank you
for passing on your love of books to me.*

BIRTHDAY NOTE +
VINCENT'S EARS + AMNESIAC

It read something like this...

I have read much. You have read much, my son. That I have passed on to you, a love for what lies on the page. Also, reverence for things we do not completely understand. I fear the Almighty. You, not as much. I give you a pass since all the reading has soiled you. I would like to think you are not an atheist but this is not the time nor the place. For now, let us bless what we have and the remaining time we have and accept the unknowable. For some things are not meant to be seen or heard. Some things need to be taken to the grave. Let us believe we have the heart to chase dreams. And that, my son, is the greatest gift.

-Happy Birthday, Your Papa

The note was written on a scrap of paper, small enough to fit within the inside lining of Vincent's wallet. The writing was barely legible. Some of the words dissolved with age.

Certain letters were half realized. The other was a ticket stub to a concert tucked in the opposite side of the wallet. The date on the ticket stub was from thirty years prior. One ticket stub. One birthday note the size of a newborn's hand. Nothing else. No money, no cards, no identification. Nothing.

A ship's horn sounded, making its way down the Tagus River and out to sea. Lisbon at dusk. Vincent sat on a bench in front of the Church of Santa Lucia. In a few minutes he would venture indoors to eat and then sleep on one of the many cots that lined the eastern wing of the church next to the rectory. It's a shelter for the homeless. It has been since the economic crash.

Later, Vincent would reread a passage or chapter from one of the pocket-sized books he carried in his one small suitcase before he would go to sleep. Only certain bits. He found he couldn't read an entire book like he used to. Sometimes, he would flip through the pages and settle on one — just to stare blankly at it. The contents of the suitcase also included a pipe and a small tin of no. 42 tobacco, reading glasses and a pinch of talcum powder. This is all that he possessed, along with the clothes on his back.

Later that evening, he could hear the head priest play the piano in the rectory. No one else could hear it, the cement walls being so thick. Vincent's ears were a gift. They were not unusually large, they just worked miraculously well. For instance, when the rest of the vagrants and other riffraff were sound asleep and he stared at the yellow ceiling, he could hear beyond the walls, beyond the Tagus spilling into the Atlantic, beyond the Azores, out into the ether and far beyond, into the outer planets whizzing past in their ellipses. At other times, he could hear a centipede crawl along a windowsill.

I am an amnesiac, the voice in Vincent's head reminded him.

I am an amnesiac, he whispered to Tristao in the cot next to his.

I don't care. No one gives a good goddamn, was Tristao's tender response. You see, Tristao was what some would call a *prick*.

Cale-se, voce pequena cadela.

You want to know the origin of your name? He asked Tristao.

Fuck no.

It basically means riotous. A calamity. You're a mess.

That all? Tristao yawned.

I could keep going if you like?

Idiota. No one likes you.

Tristao turned over, whipped his thin blanket over himself like a seasoned matador. The woman on the other side of Vincent, the one with the dreadlocks—chortled. Possibly Haitian, Vincent deduced. No one asked. Besides it was her second night in the church. Vincent thought she sounded like a seal when she laughed.

I like seals. I wish to dream about seals. I also wish—

Arrete de te parler! The Haitian hissed.

Gone was her good humor.

SIMPLE LIFE +
THREE TIMES + DEVIL'S MILK

Life was simple enough at present. This would change. A smallish man will leave Israel and travel to Lisbon. He had a vested interest to rid the world of Vincent. He had to be certain the vagrant was the one he's been seeking.

Regardless, Vincent went about his usual business of asking for loose change. Afterwards, walking in Bairro Alto, he would purchase a grilled sardinha on toasted sourdough for a bit of small change. It was cheap enough for him not to fret. It would fill him for half a day, gave him enough energy to climb and zigzag his way up dozens of steps, near Santa Lucia, where he could spy the steamers or cargo ships making their slow crawl out to sea. Most times, he would just smoke his pipe and enjoy the vanilla-tinged tobacco he was so fond of. Other times, he would nap, tired from all the walking and panhandling. If he missed dinner—which he did on occasion—he would have to wait till morning for breakfast.

Vincent went out at least three times a day. Morning,

as the bronzed hues of the Portuguese sun swept across the Tagus. Afternoon, when children and their mothers or nannies would frequent Jardim de Estrela. Evening, when the glossy squared tiles of the Rua dos Remedios seemed to be slick with rain. He would go out, wander about, panhandle for money, buy either his no. 42 tobacco or *pateis de natas*—the egg tart pastries he loved more than a good tug. Vincent was not above a good tug. Finding the right moment or spot was always the challenge for the down and out. Sometimes, you had to go for it when the opportunity presented itself. To hell with the Church warning that masturbation produces the Devil's milk! A man has certain needs.

LACKING DETAILS +
ANDRES + WARRIOR

Vincent's life lacked in the crucial details. It's been this way since the trauma. His memory or what he could remember was spotty. There was a gap in years. Many years.

Some things need to be taken to the grave.

He couldn't understand why his father wrote this. Was he European? Some mongrel? How did he arrive on the continent? Vincent's history was a jumble, like some plane's wreckage scattered about a vast sea. He tried to explain this to the Haitian.

I don't know who I am.

Who does? She replied.

I'm serious. I don't have a name.

Vous etes Vincent, she smiled her grandmotherly smile at him.

Yes, but I don't have a full name. I don't know how I arrived here.

You are so serious. *Sourire un peu.*

I've tried talking to most but no one seems to care or

want to help. Except maybe the priest.

Qu'est ce qu'il dit?

Vincent had explained it all before—visit the hall of records, stand in an airless room, hope for a friendly face, they roll their eyes, he is the butt of their jokes—there's Mr. Memory! They direct him toward Visas & Passports. Another two hours. They don't even let him approach the window. A security guard calmly escorts him out. He might face deportation. But to where, exactly? There's always the threat of deportation.

The Haitian gently grabbed his wrist and proceeded to tie a wrist-band she wove earlier next to his Chinese wristband. Her wristband was woven in the red/blue colors of the Haitian flag.

Un cadeau, she said.

She asked about his Chinese bracelet. He understood enough French to make small talk.

I found it on the street, he answered.

Dans la rue? Ca dit quoi?

I don't know what it says.

The Haitian took offense. She couldn't understand the reason to wear the bracelet if he didn't know the meaning behind the words. She became furious. Irrationally so. She rose from the cot, grabbed her soap and looked at him as if he just rolled in some shit. This was the *French* look of disgust. Vincent knew it well as a number of French vagrants did the same.

Vous etes un imbecile! She yelled as she weaved her way between the cots toward the showers.

She just called you a retard, Tristao laughed.

His sharp laugh grated on Vincent.

She didn't call me a retard.

Okay, fine—*Voce `e um retardado!*

A couple of others joined the laughter. One was a newcomer to the shelter—another Frenchman who looked Algerian. The other was Andres, a familiar face.

You're one to laugh! Tristao shouted at Andres.

Leave him alone, Vincent warned Tristao.

You're all a bunch of fools. This entire place is crawling with worms like you! He also grabbed his soap and headed to the showers.

Vincent was glad to be rid of him.

Andres was too meek to offer any resistance. He was a soft-spoken middle-aged man who lost his wife and daughter in a fire a few years back. Then promptly lost his job. The dominoes fell quickly. He was an emotional wreck. One of many who couldn't cope and ended up on the street. The government dragged him through various agencies and even admitted him to a psychiatric hospital. None of it helped. He was as raw as Vincent's feet. His trauma was of the chronic kind.

He's a pig, Vincent said to Andres. Nothing wise about that guy. The Italians would call him a *buffone.*

This prompted a slight smile from Andres. It's three simple syllables, Vincent claimed. *Buf-fo-ne.*

Il buffone! He shouted after Tristao, surprising Andres and those around him who were not used to such theatrics from Vincent. Tristao flipped him the bird as he turned the corner.

Don't you worry, Andres. You're a warrior. I have a thing with names—trust me. Your name means *warrior.*

The irony of it did not escape Vincent.

SNAKES + A STRANGER + SEALS

Vincent ran into Lucio in the Praca do Comercio amid the newly arrived throng of summer tourists, a new batch of vagrants and screaming children.

I ran into some guy who was asking about you, said Lucio.

What? Vincent paused and then asked, Who? He thought this was a joke. Lucio was the type to needle.

Some strange guy. He said he was on official business. I ran into him there.

Lucio pointed toward the statue of King Jose. Vincent glanced at the stern, bronzed figure—the horse's hooves were crushing a swarm of snakes. It was the first time Vincent noticed the reptiles.

Who was this guy? What did he look like?

Certainly not one of us, quipped Lucio.

What does that mean?

He was very official looking. Well-dressed sort.

Official? Vincent paused. A government official?

Look, I can't stand here all day answering your stupid-ass questions. Lucio paused and continued—he reeked of cologne.

Vincent turned toward the yellow buildings thinking the same man could be among the crowds next to the open-air market.

Who reeked?

The fancy fuck who was looking for you.

You know my situation!

I don't care. I don't want to care. What's in it for me?

Stop being so pervasive, Vincent pressed.

You and your fancy words. Your goddamn books! Everyone knows it's an act.

What did he ask? What did he want of me? This might be helpful. This might be—

Ay ay ay, calm down! Don't need this. Don't want this. I shouldn't have said anything.

Be decent for once! Vincent screamed.

A cluster of German tourists took notice of their heated exchange. *Filho da puta!* Lucio hissed. Don't bring attention to us! You're fucking us.

Esta bem. Esta bem. Lucio bowed to the Germans. A supplicant to possible handouts—he feigned sincerity.

Esta bem.

A screaming infant wailed. Its little feet cycled in the air above its carriage as if the little thing noticed the slithering snakes. Vagrants don't like children. Vincent was no different. They were annoyances. Please stick a bottle in that child's mouth. A pacifier. A tit. Anything. Vagrants and tramps had their own list of issues. Children were usually ignored, unless it was part of an act or to cater to a parent. Teens the same.

To the east, along the traffic-congested Av. Infante Dom Henrique, Vincent saw a man who looked like one of the new arrivals at the church. Rotund and balding, he was close to Vincent's age. He was feeding bread crumbs to a pool of pigeons gathered at his feet.

Among all the fluttering and bird-talk, Vincent noticed that Lucio slipped away. Frantically, he looked around. A possible lifeline had been cast. He shouted Lucio's name a few times. And since the infant's wailing had stopped, his voice boomed through the entire square. The German tourists muttered their disgust, then turned from him as the late afternoon sun peeked below the grey sky and struck the yellow buildings. The entire square was washed in the color of sunflowers. Everyone seemed content. He pictured seals basking in the sun. Vincent wished to feel at peace like that. Only, he didn't. He wanted his past returned to him.

FAUSTO + BUNCH
OF BASTARDS + COMPREENDO?

He was rotund, possessed a cherubic face, a gap cleaved his two front teeth. This was a new arrival to Santa Lucia. He was the one feeding the pigeons at the Praco do Comercio. His name was Fausto. He was quick to befriend Vincent. Vincent was drawn to his intelligence and sense of humor. Of course, Tristao admonished him as one of the newest arrivals.

You always warm up to the morons, don't you?

The only moron is you, Tristao.

How many helpings does he need? Tristao asked.

No one seems to complain. Only you.

God, what a pussy you are. We shouldn't push our luck. These priests give us a roof over our heads and feed us half decent food.

Stop your gossiping. No one—

Porra de gordura. The fat fuck is one of those types that will ruin it for the rest of us.

He's done nothing and he's smart. More than I can say

14

for you.

Filho da puta. Lucio is right about you.

What does that mean? A quick pause. Have you spoken with him?

Tristao didn't respond. The late afternoon light poured through the large windows. The Haitian, who always napped during this time, moaned as she turned over on her cot.

Crazy voodoo *bicha,* Tristao said.

Vincent pressed on. What did Lucio tell you? Did he mention anything?

These questions. *Estupido.* What do they prove?

It's just a question. A simple question, Tristao.

You act like this goddamn detective. What you seek is nothing. Look at me—I'm a mutt. My name is Tristao Delgado. So what? It doesn't matter. I'm a bum. No one cares. Same with you. No one fucking cares. Doesn't matter if you don't know your last name or if you had a name or if you made up a name. We're all a bunch of bastards.

The afternoon sun was in full regalia. It now burned full on from the west. Dust motes were exposed in the sunlight's entrails. Vincent's lower back was throbbing. It was probably from the numerous stairs he climbed the past week. He noticed a slight drop in weight. He also realized that Tristao was his least favorite person in the world. He couldn't stand the machismo, the constant aggression.

Why don't you talk about normal things? Tristao continued.

What did Lucio say?

I've never heard you talk about a woman. You never

mention bitches. Are you a faggot? You like dick?

Santa Lucia was like an English manor to Tristao, who never had it this good. He always said it was a stepping stone to bigger things. His next move would be huge, he boasted. He would find a way to take advantage of these troubling times.

Eu sou o cara, he said as he pounded his chest.

Vincent feared that Tristao would slash his throat while asleep. He knew he had a violent streak. Most of the long-time boarders kept clear of him. The Haitian was one of a handful who wasn't intimidated by his bullying persona.

The back pain worsened. Vincent's knees also swelled and throbbed. He needed to lessen his wandering. What he longed for was somewhere out there. But where? What? Something. Anything. He didn't have any answers.

Vincent's breathing quickened. It was the pain. It was also Tristao—the omnivore—in close proximity.

Sunlight filled the far corners of the church hall. A group of Arabs argued. Others shuffled about in slow, measured steps. Dinner would soon be served. Vincent longed to walk a bit and enjoy the river and various boats and ships making their way to and fro.

You're such an asshole, Tristao continued. I'm going to eat.

Vincent didn't respond. Instead, he faintly heard two black holes colliding in the far reaches of some universe. It is true that there are other universes, as he read during one of his library visits and testified by this slight ripple that traveled eons of time to reach him.

And don't ask me about Lucio again, Tristao's face now inches from Vincent's. He told me how you ruined it for him. We all depend on the kindness of strangers. You pull that with me and I hurt you. *Compreendo?*

Tristao turned his back and for an instant, Vincent imagined leaping at him and strangling him. Amidst the amber glow of the church hall, Vincent eased back on his cot, hands clasped behind his head and with a knowing smile further imagined the rope pulled taut, dust motes kicked up, a frenzy of glee as Tristao took his last breath, his face turning blue.

Sure, I *compreendo*, you piece of shit.

CHESS MOVES +
AMERICANS + SMALL MIRACLES

There is the Ruy Lopez, the Bishop's Opening and the Danish Gambit, said Fausto. The two men sat in the park after a long walk and a short bus ride on the Estrela line. They were fast becoming friends. Fausto couldn't stop talking even while playing chess. He was enamored by the female sex. Maybe, too much.

What I wouldn't give to sit between those two. He gestured toward two dark-haired ladies who were obviously repulsed by the vagrants. Fausto could not control his ogling and his lazy left eye did not help. He was constantly wiping it with a handkerchief he kept tucked in his shirt pocket.

He leaned toward Vincent and since he was obviously the better player and the game was near over, he whispered, I would love to stick my face between those giant tits. He let out a big laugh, enough to make the two ladies scurry away in a panic. Fausto didn't possess a filter. This was one of the qualities Vincent liked about his new friend.

Your move, he reminded Vincent.

Fausto took the last sip of his *pequeno* cafe. Always wired, he drank quickly, moved quickly, spoke quickly, his wit and observations like sagebrush catching fire. The cluster of coffee stands attracted those from all walks of life. Vagabonds and chess players and other card game junkies could sit and play all day long. It was a surety of daily life in Lisbon.

The Americans kick you out after a bit. If you don't continue buying, they will put your ass on the street, said Fausto. We wouldn't last over there.

How do you know? Asked Vincent.

This is what an old friend told me. He hitchhiked up the west coast and ended up in San Francisco. He hated it. Told me a bunch of nerds took over the city.

Nerds?

Tech geeks.

They cleared the chess board for a third game. It had become their morning ritual. Fausto was a strong player teaching Vincent new strategies, terminology and bold play.

Only bring your Queen out when you smell blood. No sooner. You need to catch the scent before you bring that bitch out, warned Fausto.

Vincent then spied two squirrels chasing one another up a tree. He followed their playful spiral until the shimmering leaves caught his attention. It put a smile on his face. A nice breeze, a full sun. Even in misfortune there can be small miracles. Fausto glanced up and saw Vincent's smile. He asked his new friend in the most matter of fact tone—What do you see, a nice pair of titties?

EGG YOLKS +
FADO + COLOR OF TAR

They raced toward the church, desperate to get in the front of line for dinner, when the younger priests were not as mindful of the portions they ladled out. The street lamps of the Rua do Paraiso flickered on for the evening. The lamps looked like egg yolks to Fausto, such was his hunger. The dinner rush at the church would be hectic, crazed, a slew of homeless jostling for position.

Vincent struggled to keep pace with Fausto. The fat man was all motion and heaving chest. His eyes crackled with purpose. His momentum rolled down the streets and avenues, across squares and parks, in front of the many churches, always crossing himself as he passed even though he never spoke of God.

The Alfama neighborhood was littered with Fado. Fado being a tradition that dated back generations. The music is the Portuguese version of *Saudade*. Vincent stood outside one spot on Rua de Santiago. The first smiling guests arrived. Various dishes caught his eye. Food samples were offered followed by tall tales and a lot of laughs—all leading to the Fadista singing melancholy songs.

Famished, both men went limp. They lost track of time and missed the dinner service at church. Both felt they entered a wormhole and came out the other end, disoriented. Vincent's legs tired. The balls of his feet were mush. He needed to save what he earned on a sturdy pair of shoes. He told Fausto to go on without him, that he would meet him back at the church. Fausto didn't respond and just kept on, disappeared from view.

Vincent sat on a stoop, a natural spot between buildings. He was content that he could rest his feet and watch couples or groups of friends enter and then spill out onto the street as the night wore on. Everyone looked young and beautiful, probably half of Vincent's age. Not one of the beautiful people noticed him.

There he sat, obviously drained, his eyes the color of tar. The smell of cooking meat blew out the vent atop the restaurant. It was not the best spot for the amnesiac. Starved, he lusted for one bite, one nibble. The prospect drove him somewhat mad. He thought of running into the restaurant to grab a handful of food but he wouldn't dare to.

So he closed his eyes and wished his bad fortunes away. He wished to go away. Far away. Swim with the seals or die and come back another person. His eyes now opened, Vincent wished to be like them — like the beautiful people who kissed and hugged, laughed and celebrated, oblivious to Vincent's suffering.

VOODOO +
TRISTAO ATTACKS + REVENGE

Tell the fat fuck to leave Andres alone. He's with us, seethed Tristao.

He's not your property, said Vincent.

No, he is my property. That's what I'm telling you.

What's this, a warning? A threat?

It is what it is.

I don't respond to threats.

I'll gut you, *seu pedaco de merda*.

The Haitian began to mumble. Her mouth and body quivered. Sensing tension, she would mumble, usually chant some island hex to protect herself from the bad spirits that were cast about. Sometimes, she would stare dead on, her eyes expressionless like dead fish.

You'd be as crazy as her if you got in my way, continued Tristao.

Fausto is not bothering anyone. Leave him out of your bullshit.

Your fat boyfriend is IN my bullshit.

We all know you're making Andres peddle your fake weed.

Keep talking, *minha amiga*. Keep it up. You're crossing the line.

He gets caught, they trace it back to you, to us, it jeopardizes our place in this church. We're all out on the street. A slight pause. You're more stupid than you seem, Vincent finalized.

In a flash, Tristao struck Vincent on the left side of his face. Half-blow, half-slap, Tristao's cupped hand fell above his left ear. An awkward blow which left Vincent stunned. Losing his balance, he fell sideways onto an empty cot. Tristao kept at him but the Haitian screamed and wildly stabbed the air with her hands. A couple of the younger priests at the other end of the hall heard the screams and ran toward the commotion. Tristao executed one final kick into Vincent's groin when he was down, then bent down saying words of warning in a seething whisper.

Next time I shank you. I swear it. I'll shank the shit out of you. Now pretend you have terrible pain, tell them you're not feeling well. Pretend!

Later, all three described their versions to the parish priest. The Haitian spoke in a frenzied manner, gestured a great deal, confused the priest with her wild eyes and manic behavior. Tristao shrugged and played it as if Vincent always had these types of episodes, this last one being the worst. He also mentioned that the Haitian was not to be trusted, that she made up crazy stories, that she might be a thief and should be watched closely.

Vincent laid low for an entire day pretending to have stomach pain. It gave him time to brew and devise a plan on how to exact revenge.

BURSITIS + KILLING
BUSINESS + HUMAN CURRENCY

A cold drizzly day as Lisbon was held captive by a grey sky. Vincent and Fausto stood under a green awning. Staying dry was key. Vincent had a red welt on the side of his forehead courtesy of Tristao's fist.

Fausto sported a new look. His head was completely shaved and buffed to a fine shine. He looked like a newly minted cue ball. A strange maneuver with the colder weather arriving, Vincent thought. At present, there were other concerns.

I wish I was there, said Fausto. I was getting this, he indicated his new look.

Tristao's going to get us kicked out. I don't trust him. He's worse than ever, said Vincent.

What's next?

I don't know.

Didn't he say he was going to stab you? Fausto inquired.

Yes.

Something needs to be done.

Any suggestions? Asked Vincent.

Go to the priest?

No way.

Do you believe him? Do you really think he's going to do it?

He's a maniac. He's a sick—

Vincent broke off and just stared at the drizzle that rippled down in waves. Both men grew quiet. This happened more often as if the change of seasons brought on more doubt about the future. This was the natural order of things—the ritual of anxiety for most vagrants. Survive the cold, new plans, new migrations, uncertainty shifting into another gear.

Jesu, I need to get laid. Fausto broke the silence. It's been too long. Too fucking long. A pause. I'm not queer, you know.

Fausto's bursitis was a nuisance. His right elbow ballooned. Hating needles, he avoided getting it drained.

There is a better life out there. It's all in the psychology of the thing, Fausto said as he grimaced in pain.

He's selling weed. Dime bags. Ever since he's been selling weed, he thinks—

Stop obsessing, Fausto offered.

I want to kill him.

Just leave. Get away from here. I'll go with you.

I want to kill him. He's a danger. Think about it, Vincent reiterated.

You're not the type. You're not in the killing business.

Fausto laughed. A nervous laugh. The mood was fast turning solemn. Both men stared ahead not focused on anything in particular.

I'll go with you. Let's leave. We can't do it immediately. Let's plan it out, keep our heads down. Let's give it to the spring, Fausto said.

Will you help me kill the asshole?

Jesu, have you a screw loose? Fausto hissed. You're a dog with a bone. Of course I've thought of it—but that's as far as it goes. The fucker has it out for me. A beat later— he cornered me in the bathroom stalls.

What? Vincent paused. The showers?

Wanted me to suck him off. Pause. I refused.

Vincent studied his friend's face and it hinted at just the opposite—a perverse look as if he did submit to Tristao's wishes—willingly.

Let me help you with the other thing, Fausto changed the subject.

What other thing?

Your past. Figuring it out. All those things you told me. Let's focus on that.

Not surprised by what he heard, Vincent knew their world was a depraved one. Tristao dealt in human currency, preyed on the weak, possibly even killed in the past.

Fausto continued. He slapped the shit out of you— you're pissed. I get it. Just focus on the prize.

What's wrong with your elbow? Vincent asked.

Ah, it's nothing. Probably the cold weather.

We need to get a hold of Lucio, Vincent said.

Lucio? He's not trustworthy.

He can help us. He has some info we need.

Bueno. Where can we find him?

Praca do Comercio.

O SUPREMO + LADIES
OF THE BECO + FIZZLE

A week passed and no sign of Lucio. Lucio did not use the church for sleep shelter or food. He had other means. A creature of the street, he peddled substances of all types, lived off his moxie. More importantly, he knew how to evade the law. Possessing a streetwise charm, he didn't traffic in certain circles and kept mostly to himself. He was a survivor.

Vincent found it strange that such a loner would team with Tristao and believed Tristao weaseled his way into Lucio's connections. The brute probably promised Lucio a major cut of whatever he promised or an important role in his newly formed group—*O Supremo*.

What's the name of their group? Asked Fausto.

The Supreme. Or something like that.

Like the music group?

Huh?

The music group, Fausto reiterated. The Supremes?

No, just Supreme. Not plural.

Sounds stupid.

That's what I thought, Vincent laughed.

Fausto kept his new look to a lustrous sheen. At times, the glare was too much. He shoplifted an emollient that he constantly rubbed onto his shiny top.

Look at this shine, Fausto would boast. I buff it, wax it, rub it—I haven't looked this young in years. I look good. Women like this look. I like this look. It'll help me get laid. It'll help you get laid. Think about it.

Fausto played chess against himself. Games that thrived on redundancy, where he catalogued specific moves over and over, often spoken out loud—the diagonals, ranks and files, Bishop to f4, Knight to e5, etcetera—certain strategies for certain situations. What would the masters do? Capablanca? Lasker? Fischer?

Vincent's eyes tired on the lookout for Lucio. They sat at the edge of the Praca do Comercio. He stretched as they were going on two hours and Fausto's constant babbling was getting to him and his legs stiffened, partly from the cold, partly from his lousy shoes.

You're walking like you have a stick up your ass, Fausto snickered.

I swear he comes here all the time.

Lucio?

Yes! There was an edge to Vincent's voice.

Relax. He'll turn up.

The asshole tells me that someone is looking for me. That the guy has the look of a government official. Then goes ahead and disappears.

Might be messing with you, claimed Fausto.

Why? Why would he go to the trouble?

Some people are fucked up. Tristao probably put him

up to it.

Really?

Sure. Look who you're dealing with.

This latest exchange worsened Vincent's irritation. More and more his thoughts turned violent. Rational or not. There were other issues that should've taken precedence, like they have for so long. An obsession began to fester. Tristao was in the way. Plain and simple. He was a menace, a wrongdoer, a fake.

There were times in the past when this type of rage welled up, overwhelmed him. He often thought this was a genetic disposition. His father being the same and his father's father.

What's running through that mind of yours? Asked Fausto.

The usual, said Vincent.

You know what I'm thinking about?

What?

Pussy, said Fausto.

My God, give it a rest!

Never. You know it to be true. You think the same. I wish I had a few extra Euros to go visit the ladies of the Beco.

As Vincent continued pacing, he thought of his last visit to the Beco, months back. Anti-climactic, guilt-ridden and some Euros later, he felt worse off than when he arrived. He saved for so long, put away little by little, only to see his penis wilt when he was alone with Flavia—his favorite. Unable to do what he so desperately wanted and needed left him feeling impotent. His manhood fizzled at liftoff. Flavia was fine enough. Her hair, lush and dark, thick like rope. She was curvy, fleshy, an enormous backside, good enough for any man. She tried to sooth Vincent, caressed his face with her long nails till his time was up. It didn't help as his shame flooded the room and spilled out onto Rua dos Remedios. Vincent has not returned to the ladies since.

SLEEP + NEW
PRIEST + LOST CHILD

It neared lights out at the church. Sleep was usually the most inviting prospect of the entire day. Similar to a dog's life, those Vincent knew slept through most of their day, the exception being Fausto. Not trusting his fellow homeless, Vincent always kept one eye open. There was gossip going round that a new priest from up north in Porto would head the church. This could change everything. The tension was barely manageable for those who already barely managed. The winds of change was evident. The younger priests were tight-lipped about it.

At least I don't have to worry about lice, Fausto said about his shaved skull.

That's true, Andres said.

This is the first time in days you've spoken to us, Vincent chimed in.

Tristao's been busy, he's selling—Andres discontinued, fearful of incriminating himself. Paranoid by nature, he didn't trust much. He definitely didn't trust the Haitian.

31

Like Vincent, he also kept one eye open. Quiet by nature, he thought that too much talking was a perversion.

Both Vincent and Fausto sat motionless on their cots. The Haitian was also seated, knitting one of her garments she sold at market. Peaceful and contemplative, the action of knitting always calmed her. It didn't seem to help Andres one bit.

No one's going to say anything, Fausto whispered, Andres' nervous energy affecting all of them.

That's easy for you to say, Andres said.

We know he's selling weed, Fausto continued. We know you're helping him.

Andres tugged at his shirt, loosened the collar, looking grossly uncomfortable. His head swiveled this way and that, the silence magnified his unease.

There's no shame in it. A man has to do whatever to get by, Vincent said.

Let's stop talking about it, Andres pleaded. *Por favor.*

Do you make decent money at least? Fausto asked.

You heard the man, Vincent tapped Fausto's arm, *ja e suficiente.*

Nao mais. E troppo e troppo. Fine. Fausto said.

The homeless spoke a variety of languages. Bits of this. Bits of that. A mongrel breed. Poor Andres, Vincent thought. The man harbored enough demons having lost his wife and child in a fire. He could barely cope. How could he manage dealing with Tristao?

What's this group Tristao's forming? Vincent asked.

I don't want to talk about it, Andres countered.

Do you want us to help you?

I don't need anything. Leave me be. I shouldn't—

Listen fuckface we are trying to be your friends, Fausto

broke in. You're mixing with the wrong people.

You have no business—

Okay okay we get it, but just know we have your back. You don't have to side with Tristao or do his dirty work, Vincent said.

I try anything, he'll make my life miserable, Andres said. He'll beat me.

The conversation came to a stop. Each man felt inclined to look in a different direction. Fausto stared at the Haitian, all the while rubbing his shiny top. Andres, true to habit, looked at his feet. Vincent glanced at the three large wooden doors of the entrance to hall where they slept, wondering if the day would come when he would step out those doors and never return. He then turned and looked at the Haitian, her eyes now shut, humming quietly and still knitting while Andres mouthed *I don't trust her* to Vincent. Fausto's rubbed his genitals vigorously while he tried to decipher what Andres just mouthed. All the noise he generated reopened her eyes.

Avez-vous des crabes? The Haitian asked.

No, I don't have crabs but I'm certain half of the folks sleeping in this church do, including the priest. Hell, Andres probably has crabs.

Est que si, fatty?

Fatty—how original, Fausto snipped. The Haitian returned to her knitting. Andres stood as uncertain as ever. Fausto still smarted at the Creole's remark, his scrotum-scratching on hold for the moment.

Have you seen Lucio? Vincent asked. Andres fidgeted, his eyes as large as his discomfort.

I told you I don't want to—

Andres, I need to speak with Lucio. It's very important,

Vincent said.

Hey, stupid—help the man out. You know his situation, Fausto added.

I've said enough, Andres threw his arms up.

Stop being such an ass, Fausto said.

Deixa-lo ser, Vincent stressed to Fausto. Stop riding him.

He's in over his head, Fausto kept at it.

Andres had the look of a whipped dog. Poor Andres, Vincent thought. He couldn't fend for himself. He survived on sheer dumb luck. Vincent was determined to throw a lifeline to his drowning friend, stand up to Tristao if need be.

You won't be alone in this, Vincent promised.

I'm not saying a word, Andres said and thought for the first time that he should turn and walk.

Lucio. Just tell me where I can find Lucio. Simple. That's all I need.

I can't make any promises. I don't know, Andres said, his voice barely above a whisper.

Bullshit. You're in thick with Tristao. Spit it out, Fausto urged and rose to his feet, a look of menace in his eyes. It was a first. Even the Haitian took notice.

Vous etres excite, fatso?

Keep out of it, you crazy loon, Fausto snapped.

I can't I can't I can't—Andres muttered.

You two knock it off. He paused.

I can't I can't I can't, Andres continued.

What's gotten into you? Vincent asked. Even the Haitian's attention turned to Andres.

I can't...

Andres backed away from the three of them. He nearly

tripped on one of the cots.

Where you going? Fausto stepped forward.

Stop pestering him! Vincent's voice boomed.

No no no no, Andres mumbled as he continued his backward weave between the cots. His voice like that of a lost child as he backed into the dark.

MORE WEIGHT +
LUCKY + I'M YOUR FRIEND

Plus de Poids.

Those were the words Fausto recently tattooed on the inside of his left forearm. *More weight.* He was the latest to join the latest trend of getting tattooed.

What does it mean? Vincent asked.

It could mean a great many things, Fausto said.

People will make fun of it.

They already do.

How did you afford that?

I know a certain someone who owed me a favor.

Ah.

The tattoo artist was from France. So, the words in French. I didn't care.

More weight? I don't get it.

It's not important that you get it. It's not meant to be gotten.

You could've just inscribed your own name.

Too obvious.

You should've gotten a tramp stamp.

Funny, Fausto responded.

A name is everything. Or, I meant to say—everything is in a name, Vincent claimed.

You have the right to think that.

You don't agree? Vincent countered.

Not really.

Your name means *lucky*.

I've never felt that. It doesn't matter. It never mattered. This matters. Fausto thrusted his newly branded forearm into Vincent's face.

Vincent is from the Latin—Vincentius. Vincens. Conquering. To overcome. It was the name of a third century martyr. A pause. But I'm certain it's not my given name.

Oh joy, Fausto cynically added.

Take it for what it's worth.

How do you know this shit?

A name is everything, Fausto. It's all we have. A brief pause. What's your given name?

It's complicated.

FAUSTO TELLS
SOME OF HIS STORY

What I do know is my mother was born in the Carpathians. She's from gypsy stock. Part Romanian, part Hungarian, maybe something else mixed in. Who knows? A true mutt. She identified more with her Romanian background. The Hungarians and Romanians really dislike one another. The entire region is full of hatred, a lot like my mother. She beat me, she thought me stupid. I have a scar on my back to prove it. As for my father, he was never around. Always traveling. The absent father. Sounds common, doesn't it? We never knew of his dealings. He was shrewd and successful in some ways. I never saw enough of him to know much more than that. Most of what I know came from his brother—Uncle Lazic. I guess you can say he was the closest thing to family that I could claim. I had a sister but she died at a young age. She died a terrible death, not something I'd like to remember. My father was a man of fine taste. He wore Italian shoes, pomaded his hair, enjoyed wearing hats. Brimmed hats. A fedora usually, never a pork pie. He thought pork pies too bohemian and he had no use for those types. Being from Budapest, he grew to be wary of bohemian culture. After a certain business trip to Russia, he never returned. Never heard from him again. He was secretive. Not easy to be around, he was of a certain type. I guess you fit people into categories. But in the end—water under the bridge as they say. Those head doctors say we are all products of our upbringing. Well, I guess abuse builds a certain type of character. I am here. I exist. I never wanted a family. Having a wife, being with a woman on a daily basis—spare me! Those types of things, I'm in over my head. The constant sex would be nice, though.

UNDERGROUND +
FRYDA + ARE YOU MY FATHER?

Grey skies skim low over Lisbon. The Tagus took on the luster of steel. It was one of the coldest winters on record. Bundled up in layers which included a sweater he found in the trash, Vincent felt the bite of scarcity. He often went underground to seek warmth along with an army of other homeless. Lisbon's metro was the new hustle and the rush for handouts turned into territorial spats. Those in need were busy bracing themselves for the winter months.

Vincent ran into those he knew and those he didn't know in this underground world. Fellow transients newly arrived or just passing through. Some developed a system over a period of time, including Vincent and Fausto, in order to maximize their earning potential. The plan was to catch the train at one end of the line, for example at Telheiras Station and ride it to the other end at Cais do Sodre. The Green Line was one of the most traveled and one developed certain strategies to wring out the most from a day. Fausto was not the best partner—felt it too exhausting to hustle like this. He would usually disappear halfway through the day. When questioned where he went, he went quiet.

Sometimes, Vincent and Fausto would exit at the Martim Moniz or Baixa-Chiado stations. These were central locations with more activity, more bustle. During his underground travels Vincent noticed those he knew or those he was in competition with.

There was Afonso. Afonso boasted that he came from nobility. He was lying. He suffered from *delusion tremens*. He was young with greasy hair and decaying teeth. A cigarette never far from his lips, he smelt like burnt toast. His favorite book was *Livro do Desassossego* by the Portuguese writer Pessoa. He could quote passages and lines from memory usually followed by a deep gaze down at his feet.

There was Donato. An arrogant son of a bitch, Fausto claimed. He was pudgy with the eyes of a rat. He was a northerner and boasted folks north of Coimbra were much kinder than the lowly southerners. Lisbonites are scum, Donato would say. We would respond, "Go back from where you came." Donato cited Elvis Presley as an influence. When asked what kind of influence, he responded a *life influence.*

There was Emilio. Emilio was an edgy sort who always looked for a fight. Highly competitive, he behaved as if sections of the Green Line were his domain. He would intimidate others as if he were a Mongolian warlord. He was smallish. Not midget-sized small but Napoleon-sized small. *Little Man's Syndrome.* During the summers he went shoeless. During the colder season he had no choice but to protect his feet. He refused to wear shoes, wrapping newspaper or other fabric and knotting it up around his ankles. He felt shoes too constricting.

There was Gabrielo, the Pious One. Gabrielo was a man of faith. His head buried in the Bible, he peppered his days with Christian rhetoric—*There are wolves within, and there are sheep without* or *He that becomes protector of sin shall surely become its prisoner.* Quiet and devout, he was the ideal of the repentant sinner. Many of the homeless thought him phony. He was too good, too lofty. *Luz brilha brilhante,* people would complain. They found his forgiving nature a disgrace. Many didn't give him a chance.

I don't want to hear his bullshit, Fausto griped.

There was Fryda, keeper of the peace. A stout woman in her seventies with lively eyes and cropped hair, she walked with a severe stoop. A small Beagle was her companion. The dog's name was Gertrude, an old bitch with bad hips and one lame eye. The dog conjured sympathy amongst strangers and community alike. Fryda was usually found seated, her bent frame too awkward to stay upright. She sat mostly on a subway bench and claimed it as her own. Next to them was a shopping cart with their heap of belongings -plastic bags, backpacks, a tarp and a piece or two of luggage. Fryda had a calming effect on the tribe, if one could call it that. Many quarrels were resolved by simply going to see her or just being in her presence. She was respected like a deity. It was quite possibly a sense of home she created wherever she camped, accepting one and all, without judgement or vice.

There was Hilario and Gil. Brothers, but not by blood. Hilario was the joyful type. Gil was his counterpart. He followed Hilario around dutifully. With a wisp of chin hair,

Gil looked like a goat. His angular cheeks and wide-set eyes added to the resemblance to the farm animal. While Gil was clearly the follower, Hilario was the rockstar. Those around him would be in stitches or held rapt by his storytelling charm. In these moments, Gil would normally be off to the side, shoulders slumped, his baggy clothes draped to the floor, his jealous eyes glued to Hilario's fans.

As Vincent reflected on others who shared his quandary, his mind wandered and eventually settled on a recurring dream of his. He recalled a restaurant, an open-air restaurant, with a view of the night sky. At the head of the table was an older man. Frail, dark sunken eyes, with silver wisps of hair riding crescents around his ears. Vincent assumed this man was his father but his features were never too clearly defined. Who else could it be? He sat there, this old man—motionless—with Vincent seated to his left. Around them was a teeming restaurant full of smiling, laughing people. It was always very loud.

Vincent could never remember who else was seated at the table. And never did the old man look directly at Vincent, his eyes just focused on the heap of food which sat untouched before them. As Vincent looked beyond the table not one of the dozens of patrons ever looked at him or this old man. Not once. What he did see were the waiters running crazily down two parallel aisles with enormous plates of food balanced on their arms.

The old man seemed content with his own thoughts. His only action was the drinking of his black tea. Oblivious to all the bustle, every now and then, the old man would grab a sugar cube to place in his mouth.

It's the way of the world! Someone at the table blurted out. Another said in monotone, Bergen-Belsen, Dachau,

Buchenwald. It came off like a chant. Another yelled, What strange names! These strangers were just that, appeared out of the blue.

Vincent sat there completely disoriented.

The little thing is actually a big thing, someone else blurted out.

I can barely get up in the mornings, someone else added.

What?? Vincent asked desperately, still trying to put two and two together in regards to the strange names already mentioned.

I can barely get it up in the mornings.

Get up? GET IT UP? What are these people saying??

Amongst all the talk and activity, Vincent turned his head skyward to locate one star which burned bright.

It's due to the light pollution, the old man spoke.

What? Vincent asked, still uncertain the old man uttered anything since he sat quiet like some wounded animal the entire time.

Bergen-Belsen, Dachau, Buchenwald. The old man spoke these names in monotone—carefully, deliberately.

The names did not trigger any reaction from Vincent as if his amnesia prevented him from making any connection in the dream as well. Instead, both Vincent and the old man sat like stone figures amid the frenzy of movement and loud talk. One in a state of perplexed disbelief, the other in a state of wounded introspection. Through it all, one thing Vincent never asked, never got around to asking—*Are you my father?*

LICE + SHANKING + FUCKED UP

There was a lice outbreak at the church. Fausto spotted some nits on Vincent as they argued about the fat man's Houdini act in the middle of the day. As usual, Fausto evaded or changed the subject every time it was broached. Tristao was besides himself as he accused everyone in sight for the outbreak, even accusing the bald Fausto.

I'm bald, Fausto said nonchalantly. Don't be stupid.

Foda mudo, Tristao seethed. You don't know anything. You rummage in the trash around Martim Moniz among the rats and bring that filth back here. They're crawling in your pubes!

First off, I don't rummage in trash. Secondly, I hope you and your little *cadelas* aren't spying on me. Thirdly, you're stupid, so don't compare my intelligence to yours.

Andres meekly attempted to hold Tristao back knowing another brawl inside the church would spell the end for all of them.

You talk a big game, fatty. Yes, keep talking. Surrounded by your friends, you're a real big man. Just know, your time will come.

Your threats are useless. You're useless, Fausto responded with a seeming indifference. Also, stop bossing Andres around and making him sell your fake weed. He wants nothing to do with you.

Andres refused to look Tristao in the eyes whose jugular veins ballooned to the size of ropes. Enraged, he was ready to pounce. His nostrils pulsed and he began grunting.

Fausto, enough.

Vincent spoke. Seated on the cot draped in a plastic tarp, the Haitian was ridding his hair of lice. Meticulous and with great care, she combed and cleaned strands of his scalp, working her way clockwise from left to right.

Vincent also averted Tristao's eyes. He made a vow not to speak to him unless he was forced to. No one looked at Tristao since it would further enrage him. The Haitian was too busy with the treatment to look. She hummed to herself and wasn't fazed by all of this. Vincent came to realize she was the most sensible of the group. She was strange but there was something tender and charming about her strangeness.

Let's all take a breath, Vincent said. Fausto, it's no use. Leave it.

Yes, leave it you fat fuck, Tristao said. You crossed the line.

Always the cornered animal, Tristao glanced back and forth between Fausto then Vincent and back between them a few times as if deciding who would be the first to get shanked as they cleared the stairs at Martim Moniz.

And if you want to talk to Andres, you go through me, Tristao said, spittle flying from his mouth.

You can leave now. Fausto said. A burst of rare

machismo as he stood. Whatever inspired him quickly gave way to a feeling of fear as he made the mistake of looking Tristao directly in the eyes.

The Haitian stopped what she was doing. Vincent could hear the cold blood rush through Tristao's veins. With a killer's certitude, he stepped back and conveyed, you're either with me or not, stand against me and pay the price. He was being true to his Manichean self.

Fausto sweated heavily. He realized that he stepped in it. A lump formed in his throat. He began to cower, shift in place. This did not escape Tristao—the scent of fear. It oozed out of Fausto.

Tch tch tch...*bem, bem*. Okay, okay. Tristao spoke. We will not settle it here. We will settle it beyond these walls. I let it go for now. Sure. Sure, fatso. *Sem problemas*. No problem. You will live to see another day.

Shaken, Fausto's courage was now ill-defined. I fucked up, I fucked up, he thought. Some words were said by others but became distorted. He fell into a coward's trance.

Vincent spoke up seeing the doom on his friend's face.

Let's stop all this. We need to be very careful. No more of this.

And still, both Tristao and Vincent refused to look at the other, their genuine dislike like a constant game of cat and mouse.

Vincent continued. We still don't know what's going on here at the church. You've heard the rumors. They're probably bringing in an older guy. A hardliner. We have to make a good impression. Stop all the bickering. We need to be careful. Fausto, *nao mais*.

Tristao was still locked in on Fausto. The fat man was too scared to move. The flutter of pigeons punctured the silence. Tristao winked at Fausto then gestured to Andres to leave. Fausto unclenched his fists, revealed his clammy hands. The Haitian continued her work on Vincent's hair. Trailing Tristao, Andres turned round and gave a helpless look to Vincent who shook his head slightly, a gesture of disappointment since he felt powerless to help.

The Haitian began humming once again.

MINT +
HERNANDO'S FEET + COMET

Vincent's hair smelled like mint. Fausto commented on it while complaining of his real name of Frederick, his birth name, which he would speak of later. The minty smell brought a smile to the Haitian's face. Maybe she found her calling as caretaker, provider, godmother. She found allies in Vincent and Fausto. This was no small feat in the homeless community.

So they hunkered down. Their travels outside the church slowed to a minimum. Vincent noticed that he was thinning, Fausto just the opposite. He still went out—his forays a seeming success—witnessed by his widening girth. He reminded Vincent of an animal fattening itself for the winter. Fausto played the game, whatever game it was.

Everyone inside the church played the game, including these men of God. These *solemn* men who wanted nothing more than to watch porn and stroke a vagina. Yes, they played their parts, Vincent bitterly thought.

Flat on his back, Vincent turned to notice Fausto lying on his side, his knees slightly tucked so his feet wouldn't dangle over his sunken cot. Vincent turned in the other direction to see the Haitian also on her side, her dreads draped over her face as she snored lightly. He also noticed a horrible smell, probably coming from Hernando's feet, his bandaged wounds now beginning to fester and turn rank. Hernando would need to attend to this or be asked to leave, infections like this not being tolerated. The homeless were not given much leeway in these matters.

The priest played his piano. The sound conveyed a sense of departure, a farewell. Each stroke of the keyboard as light and careful as the previous touch. In his mind's eye, Vincent could see the priest, his hands lifting above the keys, lifting as if it would keep lifting, only to be drawn back to the instrument.

He continued playing. Each note lingered more than the previous. The man and this instrument produced the most beautiful sound. Vincent couldn't move. His body did not belong to him. It was a force beyond him. The bliss belonged to the priest and the priest alone. Vincent imagined him in one of those moments which a musician or an artist can only experience, a moment that is rendered obsolete once it passes. Born in the moment, disappears in the same.

Time passed and with it the last note the priest played. It lifted above the church and into the night sky, past the stratosphere, into black space, mixing with the cocktail of inert gases, then among the local group of planets, only to join with one of the comets that Vincent could hear as it streaked on its million-year path.

VIGILANT +
NO FRIENDS + IGNACIO SILVA

As Vincent cleared the steps from Martim Moniz looking for Fausto, a man approached him from behind, took him by surprise.

You need to watch yourself. Someone is after you.

Vincent turned swiftly. He was shocked to see Lucio standing there.

You need to be more vigilant.

I thought I'd never find you.

Lucio smirked, You didn't. I found you.

The morning fog lifted. The seasonal weather had an adverse effect on the populace. Stern faces all around.

Word on the street is that you're ignoring Tristao and acting tough. Lucio said. He doesn't like to be ignored.

Him and his stupid, silly games. I'm sick of him.

He has it out for you, *minha amiga*. As well as the fat man.

I thought you were with him. Part of his stupid group.

Lucio smiled broadly, I'm with no one. I'm with myself.

With that, Vincent turned to scan his surroundings. His eyes darted about.

Nervous? Lucio asked.

About what?

About anything?

I'm looking for a friend, replied Vincent.

O homem gordo? Lucio let out a brief laugh. The fat man is not your friend.

Whatever.

Like me, like you, like everyone—we have no friends. He's in it for himself. Just like you.

Shimmers of sunlight knifed through the Lisbon sky. A mosaic of grey was a constant at this time of year. It's one of the defining features of the city and its pervasive melancholy. Outside of Martim Moniz and other central areas, the seemingly empty streets (you could turn a corner and find yourself very much alone), was a city for lovers. The growing homeless population seemed to intrude on this lover's paradise. With an old world feel - it's decaying buildings, hilly streets and aging tramlines - Lisbon had a mesmeric effect on those in love or those searching for love.

You need to break yourself of your habits, Lucio said.

What does that mean?

If someone wants to harm you, which someone does, you need to mix it up a bit, *estupido*.

Tristao wouldn't dare.

It's all he thinks about, Lucio warned. He has a one track mind. More the fatty, than you. But still, he doesn't like you.

I thought all he cares about is his weed empire. Besides, how's Andres?

Why do you have such a hard-on for that loser?

Why does Tristao need him?

Because he will do anything Tristao asks, Lucio said.

The sunlight was doing a tango of sorts, either stepping forward or stepping back into the grey. Both Lucio and Vincent glanced about, their none-too-friendly conversation on hold. After a few moments of silence, Lucio spoke.

This place is like a ghost town.

You're not one for small talk, Lucio. Not feeling well?

Pedaco de merda. I'm here to tell you that the man who sought you out was from out of town.

Out of town?

Yes.

From where?

I don't know.

Why didn't he just come to the church? Vincent asked.

How the fuck should I know? Maybe he didn't want to climb all those goddamn steps and hills to get there.

What exactly did he say?

He mentioned you. He mentioned his name. He looked suspect.

You're not giving me much useful information, here.

Listen, dumbfuck—you're such a hard head—a stupid dumbfuck that doesn't know any better. This stranger approaches some of us, most turn their backs. He's not one of us. He asks a few more times if anyone knows you. I mentioned I knew you. I shouldn't have but I did. You know the type—the official type—they don't belong but I stood forward, not actually forward, but I said yes, I know you. Fucker walks to me, tells me his name, his stupid ass name and fuck him I say when he turns to leave, fuck him, you know. We don't like the type but still I said yes.

Lucio seemed exhausted, almost forlorn after this attempted explanation. Vincent had never seen that particular look on his face. Strangely, it seemed as if Lucio was reaching out, proved that he somewhat cared.

Always the damp. Always the chill. For now, Vincent's body seemed to warm at this new prospect. The scent of promise. It did warm him. The back of his neck, the hollow of his back, his smallish hands, all tingled with expectation as if he found himself at the front of a long line, in front of all others who wanted to be where he now stood.

Does this man have a name? Asked Vincent.

Silva, Lucio said.

Silva?

I think he said, Ignacio Silva.

CONSIDER MYSELF LUCKY

You want to talk names, let's talk names. My father's name was Frederick. *Frigyes* in Hungarian. One day when I was growing up he told me in these exact words—*I bequeathed my name unto you*. Bequethed was the fanciest word he'd ever spoken. Of course he was a bastard. *Desgracado*. Not a true bastard but one in spirit. My grandfather named my father Frederick. My grandfather was a great admirer of Frederick the Great, the Prussian monarch. His name meant *peaceful* or more specifically, *peaceful ruler*. A monarch, a man who had been deemed 'Great' by his admirers, who has had a hand in wars and thousands of deaths and his name means *peaceful*. Ironic shit. The man was radical. He was a homosexual and an atheist. Can you imagine? The monarch, standing elbows out, eyeing and then fucking his young officers! I tell you, it's a crazy world. This guy never had much faith in religion, thought it similar to voodoo. He had balls.

I didn't hate my father. The man, like I said, was *desgracado*. I wish it were different. And so he passes his name onto me. It's a name. Simply, just a name. But a name is everything—just ask those damn celebrities or famous writers—and besides, I had my own path to pave. I wanted the freedom to choose. Frederick is a name for Prussian fags! I wanted a sense of witchery, to feel the power of sorcery. So, I chose Fausto—a slight change from Faustus. I didn't want a rip-off of the name or the legend. I have made no pact with the devil. Nothing that extreme. I have made this choice. I had to reinvent myself.

So, I survive and survived a cold house with very little love. I went another way. I consider myself lucky.

VINCENT'S EXECUTIONER

It is a day like any other day. It's morning. Early morning.
You rise. Sometimes the mind still lingers in the throes of
sleep. The body, your nerves, they do what it must do.
They function. The physics of movement obey certain
signals. Some more than others. Some are sluggish. Some
are feverish. Some trance about at a leisurely pace, letting
the day unfold like a dream. Sometimes you wake, still in
the grip of that dream, a particular dream, maybe a dream
which recurs like a needling motif. You wake, relieved that
you are not an actor who doesn't know his lines for
Opening Night. You dream this particular dream,
regularly. You are an actor (in the dream) who walks
around knowing that you will be performing on stage later
that evening and you don't know your lines. The
performance comes as a surprise to the one that dreams
it. People are counting on you. There will be an audience
that is paying money to see you. You supposedly have been
rehearsing for weeks only to find yourself clueless –
practically mute. You walk around in the dream like some
invalid. You walk aimlessly. Where are you going? The

anxiety begins to manifest. You fret. You think of escape but the dream entraps you. Strangely, no one in the dream, the others you encounter, ever mention the performance yet you walk around with the burden. A very private burden.

And you wake. Your eyes blink. The morning light greets you. You realize that you are free, that you are no longer ensnared in the nightmare. Relief. You continue with your morning rituals. You then find yourself out on the streets. You walk down Campo Santa Clara, heading toward Calcada Cascao. You head west. It is early morning. Fog, maybe low flying clouds or a mix of the two. A brisk wind whips up debris and trash. It means the left side of your face will be colder than your right unless you turn your entire face south toward the river. You know this river. It feels like home. You then descend down a flight of steps, one of many, which connect the tiered streets of the Alfama. One thing you notice as you look up at the tiled roofs and whitewashed homes are the lines of wash which are strung between buildings or draped over terraces.

Calcada Cascao then dumps you out onto Rua dos Remedios. It is here, at this corner where you are greeted with the eternal verities of daily life—um cortado, pasteis de natas, torrada or toast, fatias douradas (similar to French toast). The healthy aroma of fresh baked bread, pao, of finely brewed espresso—um italiano, um bica, um garoto—where you find men leaning on counters, some boisterous, some not so much, some reading a half-folded paper, some discussing the previous evening's futbol match, some smiling, some bent over by the weight of the economic slump.

A decision needs to be made. Either continue down

Rua dos Remedios or head in the opposite direction on Calcada do Forte. Down R. dos Remedios is Ephraim's Bakery. It's on the corner of Beco do Surra. Ephraim's father, Jaime, opened the bakery after apprenticing for some years with a baker by the name of Oswaldo. Of course, working for his father, Ephraim continued the family trade. The smell of fresh *pao* as captivating as the taste of the ripest guava. Heading south on Beco do Surra is a flight of stairs which never seems to end. Patience and stamina are needed. The patience of a seaman or the stamina of a runner. It eventually leads to R. Jardim do Tabaco. You are now closer to water. The salty water flows inland far enough to fill the air with its hint of promise. Anything as vast as the Atlantic carries with it the hint of promise.

R. Jardim do Tabaco is lined with snack bars, markets, farmacias, shoe-menders, haberdashers, fado. In warmer weather the street is a feast for the eyes, an organ of activity. If the sun is merciless and the streets are drenched in Lisbon's citrine light, you can duck into Cafe Teatro Santiago Alquimista. Like many of its kind, it's marked by its tiled numbers above the door or double doors and you step into what seems like a hollow until your eyes acclimate. You begin to define shapes, the lamps begin to cast their own artificial light on the wooden floors, for there is wood everywhere—inlaid along the walls, tables, bar, the beams above one's head. There is a sense of home, where one can feel safe, hide from one's pursuers or warm oneself or lean one's head against the cool brick walls. For Cafe Teatro Santiago Alquimista feels subterranean.

Peeking in as you pass outdoors is not the same as

actually stepping into its cool shroud, the innards of the place beguiling you with its charm. You find a seat, a small wooden table in the corner, possibly with one of the velvet curtains draped close and you probably would have a glass of sangria or a vinho verde in hand. It would be quiet, before the night-time rush but then again if it is winter, something warm will do. An um cortado, possibly.

Once comfortable, you look around, the place has the feel as your own personal space. You bask in the warmth and the little corner you carved out. The waiter not caring how long you stay, his head buried in a magazine or paper. The place has no definite hours, it is open every day, all year round it seems. Again, it is the warmth you crave, the first touch of the warm drink to your lips. Or a sherry, accompanied with a little bowl of olives—a courtesy in some places—will usually bring a smile to a man's face.

It is difficult to break away from this. The outside world not being so kind. The only thing that could help are the dreams you have. Or it could be something you do not yet possess. Besides your clothing, the newsboy cap you wear, to the overcoat and scarf that you wrap tighter as it gets colder, the one thing that drives you is that one thing you do not yet possess. It is the secret which belongs to history. It is the secret of the people whom you once loved, of those who died and those who are still searching, as you are for them. It is the tingle in your fingertips. Your fingertips are prone to this tingling.

And always the fear. Of never knowing. Or knowing too much.

These are the streets Vincent walked, the same sights and smells. Round every corner, round every bend, he knew these streets. He knew where he could get a small handout or where to settle into a small corner. He knew these little places, he knew them all. It was a time to bundle up, to wait it out. He knew not to push it, to overdo it or take advantage of kindnesses.

The Jew marked these same streets. He arrived in Lisbon to begin his pursuit. This little man was Vincent's willing executioner.

MIDGET CONDOM +
KILLED BEFORE + PUPPET PLAY

You're telling me that the valves will be shut off?

That's what I'm hearing.

Who's telling you this?

People talk. The young priest seems to have accepted it.

Why do you say that?

He seems defeated. Resigned.

Do you really think it's going to happen?

I don't know, Fausto. My instincts tell me yes.

Vincent and Fausto walked side by side around the large square outside the Baixa-Chiado station. Vincent noticed some stubble on Fausto's head.

I see your hair is growing back.

My head is as cold as a witch's tit. I'll shave it off again. In summer.

You of all people can't get a hat?

I'll tough it out. It builds character.

I told you, you could borrow my other hat. The one I

found.

It doesn't fit. It's like putting a midget-sized condom on my dick.

Both men laughed. It was hearty enough to bounce about off the empty square. Lately, there wasn't much to laugh about. They would be lying to themselves if they thought there were good times ahead. Scraping by—if one could call it that. Handouts were scarce. They were not spending so much time together, having other things on their minds—getting through the winter, surviving the possible change at the church, the 'valves being shut off' - that's what Fausto referenced earlier. A stricter regime. Less tolerant. There was talk of bringing in a traditionalist, someone who would put the homeless to work to earn their keep.

I haven't seen Tristao lately, Fausto said.

Neither have I.

I guess that's a good sign.

I guess.

You don't think he's up to something?

He's always up to something.

Do you think he's serious?

About what?

His threats. About coming for us.

I don't know, he's unpredictable, a psychopath. I'm sure he's killed before.

Fausto became uneasy, his insides stirred. His smile changed to a look of concern. He rubbed his stubbled head with his sausage-shaped fingers. Fausto's worry carried over to Vincent, both now bound in dread.

They walked in silence, both men peered in different directions. Fausto looked due north toward the Teatro

Nacional D. Maria, noticing its familiar colonnade. Vincent also looked toward the theatre and couldn't remember the last time, if ever, he saw a performance. Such was his amnesiac mind. He sensed the theatre to be a place of magic.

In his early days in Lisbon after a bout of drinking, Vincent usually remembered bits and images of a puppet play presented by street performers. What Vincent recalled was the story of a young man who eventually returned home after a long absence. He imagined the puppet that was the character of the young man, after a series of humiliations, stuck in a land in which he did not recognize. He was at a loss at how he arrived there, at that place, at that time in his life. The people embraced him. He even fell in love, eventually losing his love on an ocean voyage, as she toppled over the railing as he was taking a photo, lending some absurdity to the story he made up in his mind. Through sheer dumb luck, some stroke of lightning, he found a clue of where he came from and fought tooth and nail to return to that place. Vincent believed there to be some religious connection with the story and asked Fausto if he heard of it.

I have no fucking clue, the fat man said, looking preoccupied.

Both men walked on. They peered into stores and shops and noticed only a trickle of people. Some cafes had outdoor heat lamps. They passed the center fountain which still gushed water. The spray undulated in their direction mirroring the wave pattern of the tiles they walked on. The two men looked for their own, fellow transients in an area which usually crawled with them.

Nada.

For a brief moment, they found themselves to be in an alien place thinking strange, abstract thoughts. On the horizon nothing was clear or distinct, their minds mirrored what their eyes saw.

Fausto broke the silence of this strange episode.

Remember weeks back when you asked me to help you with that thing?

What thing?

The thing with Tristao.

What thing??

About getting rid of him.

I remember.

Well, I'm in, Fausto said.

FORTUNES CHANGE +
SINTRA + GIVE OR RECEIVE

Fortunes change. Fausto was feeling that. He succumbed to irrational thoughts. His mind was swamped by fear. He felt he had to protect himself. Arm himself. As he peered into a half liter milk bottle he was drinking (more on this later), the creamy white residue at the bottom reminded him of the white clouds of Sintra. A thick, gossamer white. The town itself was ridiculously colorful. There was a Moorish castle, the ruins of a former monastery, Roman monuments (it was said that Caesar was stationed there for a time). The town was awash in red yellow and pink— a mix of Roman and Arab influences.

It is said the fog never lifts in Sintra. On the day Fausto recalled it was quite the opposite. He was on his way to Lisbon after a brief stay in Graz. Fausto's view atop the town was striking. He looked up at a blue sky. A deranged blue. And then peered down at the murkier blue of the Atlantic. From his vantage point, it seemed as if the entire town were either sliding or climbing into the vastness of both. All around were hills and ravines, a natural barrier from the barbaric tribes the Romans once battled. At the time, atop the heavenly view, Fausto didn't want to relive the lewd act he had to perform for a spot on an already packed train from Porto.

He did the same for the bottle of milk he held. Fausto had to get by. Make do. Do what he had to do. No smiles. No *obrigados*. The milk came at a price courtesy of Hector, the owner of the grocery store whom Fausto sucked off an hour prior. Zipping up his fly, he told Fausto to grab the milk and make himself scarce. Fausto loved his milk. And has since childhood.

Can I use the head before I go? He asked the grocer.

Get the fuck out before I call the cops, Hector seethed.

Hector was a *bunda* to those who knew him. Married and a father of three, he sought cock on the side. He frequented a couple of underground spots where he ran into Fausto.

It's near the Baixa-Chiado metro stop, he said. It's called *Hector's*. It's my name, he smiled and boasted with a swollen chest. He was a bear of a man.

Swing by one day. You like to give or receive, *minha amiga?*

KNIFING + PANDORA'S
BOX + DO WHAT YOU MUST

A transient was knifed outside the church. The man was transported to the nearest hospital, his life in the balance. Rumors were rampant. There was talk that Tristao knifed the poor sap. Drugs were possibly involved. Money owed or money not delivered. Not seen at the church lately, Tristao became a ghost. There was talk that he shacked up with a young girl in her late teens, bartered his bad weed for lodging and sex. Some say that the imminent change of the church leadership scared him away. The head priest, the young man who played piano late into the night, was abnormally tight-lipped about the knifing. In the past, there would be gatherings, a sermon, a stern talk to certain individuals. Not this time. It seemed his own heart betrayed the young priest. The weight of his very own papacy in danger he avoided the other priests and his congregation. Most things did not feel right to all involved.

Getting laid will cure many of our ills. It will put us at ease, Fausto said to Vincent as they walked after dinner on

Campo Santa Clara. The dome of Santa Lucia to the south, a pink strip of sky outlined its features.

Don't you agree? Fausto continued.

Is that all you can think of?

What else is there to think of?

You're fucking incredible!

Don't act like you're above it, *minha amiga*. You could use a lay in the worst way.

A man gets knifed outside the church and this is what you talk about?

What's the use?

The use??

Of speaking about it. Does anyone really care? Nothing's is being done. Nothing will be done. Do you see any officials, any police asking questions, acting like they care? Fausto listed.

So his life doesn't mean anything?

A man like us?

Yes.

A man like us??

Yes! What's the matter with you?

A stretch of silence. It was dark out. An older woman, squat and stout, followed by her husband, also on the stout side, stepped out of a pastelaria across the way. He walked with a cane, she with a heavy shawl and short, shuffling steps. She carried a boxed cake they just purchased. They weren't in any rush at this time of day. That would be sacrilegious. Ask any Portuguese. Vincent was the exception.

Why are you so worked up? Fausto asked.

It's nothing.

Tell me.

Nao e nada.

It must be something, Fausto pressed.

You get worn down, that's all.

From what?

From it all.

Exactly, that is why we must grab hold of a nice pair of titties and ride into the sunset!

Are you covering something up? All this talk of—

Vincent caught himself. They rounded a corner and the light went with it. Campo Santa Clara now just street lamps, glossy tiles and poorly lit shop signs. Half the shops closed early due to the recent crisis. The two men noticed another pair of vagrants on the opposite side of the street. Neither pair acknowledged the other. Gone was the pink sky, now replaced with a dark violet, along with the flickering lights. Looking at this, one could see why Libson could lull someone into a trance. Both men entertained finding a nice bench with a good view, the warmer weather inviting them to doze off. Instead, they continued bickering.

Finish what you were going to say, Fausto said.

You don't want to hear it.

I want to hear it.

I know where you go. I know what you do, Vincent said.

What does that mean?

When you go above ground. Near Baixa. The market.

So...?

I know WHAT you do.

Fausto slowed to a crawl. Vincent slowed with him. The fat man eventually stopped.

What is it I DO? Fausto asked in a deliberate way.

It doesn't matter. I know.

Vincent wished to keep walking. Fausto spoke.

You're talking in circles. You speak nonsense. Tell me, what do you know?

Vincent looked at Fausto for a few, long, deliberate moments. He was charting an unknown path. He decided against opening Pandora's Box even further.

Nada.

Everything is nada with you. Speak up. Tell me.

I'm not here to judge. It's not my place.

You followed me?

No.

Bullshit.

Lucio told me.

Vincent noticed a look in Fausto's eyes he'd never seen. The tranquil evening gave way to a river of manure. Vincent walked into it—stupidly.

Lucio? You friends with him now? Fausto snapped.

Acalme-se.

Calm down? Heed your own advice, minha amiga.

Making threats now?

It is what it is.

I meant nothing, Vincent said.

Sure you did. You meant something. You're accusing me of something.

I told you, it's nothing. I shouldn't have spoken. I'm dealing with my own—

Are you in tight with Lucio?

What?

Are you with THEM?

Them? What—what??

What have you seen? Tell me! What have you seen!

Like boxers swinging wildly, both men kept at it— nearing empty.

That's enough. Calm down! You're besides yourself, Vincent said with gritted teeth.

Fausto stopped. For a brief moment, he stopped. His body went limp.

Acalme-se. Just stop for a second. I'm not tight with anybody. Lucio found me. He told me of that guy from the Records Office, Vincent explained.

You're lying.

I'm not lying, asshole.

What are you accusing me of, then?

It's not for me to say.

You might as well. Spit it out.

Leave it.

Is it that I suck dick? Fausto blurted out.

Pandora's Box opened. Vincent didn't respond. Nothing he said would have made any difference. Violet sky, yellow street lamps, a few stars burning to their ultimate ruin. Vincent acknowledged, as well as he could under the circumstances, that this was something he would never utter. It was the unspoken covenant of the homeless—*Do what you must.*

FAUSTO NOT SPEAKING +
KIKI + WHALE'S UNDERSIDE

Vincent felt a moment of peace. It seemed like ages. Of course it wasn't all true—the ridiculous notion that all is well even at the best of times. At present, Fausto was not speaking to him after their blowout on Campo Santa Clara. Vincent heard him boast of moving on once the weather warmed. Possibly to Brussels or Amsterdam. He made certain Vincent heard every word. He hadn't moved to another cot, even though it was possible to do so. Fausto was conversing with a new arrival. She was an extremely large woman with enormous ankles and feet. She had dyed hair, close-cropped, the color of sunflowers. Several earrings rimmed her left ear. She had small breasts, completely disproportionate to her size. Tattoos were etched on her arms, thighs, ankles. There were toe rings on her plump toes. Her name was Kiki.

It was Kiki's first night at the church. The Haitian's cot was available. She left the day after the knifing. This was often the case. The transients came and went. Nothing said, nothing seen. Vincent would be lying if he claimed he was not hurt by the lack of a proper goodbye. They were not the closest of friends but there was a tacit understanding that grew between them. She somewhat understood him, his predicament, his lack of a true name and history. The Haitian was strange. Strange enough to be *thought* strange. Maybe that is what they shared.

Vincent longed for his favorite tobacco. A nice, full tin of No. 42. He had not visited his favorite *tabaco* shop in some time. The season had been difficult. There was the killing (the man outside the church and there would be more)—the forgotten to join the ranks of the truly forgotten.

And once again Vincent stared upwards at the ceiling, goaded by the young pastor's playing. Knowing his music, it sounded like Rachmaninov but he wasn't certain. He heard the distinct tinge of Russian melancholy, the complexity and scale of keys climbing on top of one another. Muffled sneezes and coughing interrupted his listening.

The Great Fucking Hall of Snores!

He did not belong here stuck among the delusional, mad, the rotten and rotted out. The gangrene, the pus, the open cankers, the neglected wounds—both physical and mental. He could list a thousand terrible things, but why? He tried to think good thoughts.

He closed his eyes to wake in his own flat. Vincent imagined making a fried egg with a toasted baguette, possibly some jam spread upon it and a steamed cafe com leche. There would be a bookcase filled with books. Big windows, lots of light. And once or twice a year, for special occasions, he would purchase a newly published hardcover book. He would take the new book on the subject of Cosmology or Roman History or one of the world wars and he would take it with him on his morning walk to the park or along the river—its surface as smooth as a whale's underside (or that's what Vincent imagined the underside of a whale to be). He acquired a bench, sat erect, the book cradled against his chest. He was proud to be able to own it, hold it, feel its weight in his hands. He realized how lucky he was, eventually sitting the book on his lap and lighting his pipe before he cracked the book open. He further imagined returning home, a bottle of wine, a hearty meal and making love to the woman he loved.

Vincent felt his chest constricting. Bad thoughts resurfaced. At times, he wished he were dead, such was his anguish. So did the Jew.

WITCHING HOUR

Another homeless man was found stabbed. The victim was found with his pants down at his ankles and possibly violated by the looks of it. Here is what a newspaper article wrote about the stabbing the next morning.

An unidentified African male, possibly in his late 30s was the victim of a stabbing and possible rape. The victim was found by a group of Chinese tourists at the Jardim Julio de Castilho. A popular tourist spot, with an incredible view of the city. The slumped body rested against the wall underneath the blue-tiled panels that depicted the Christian attack on St. George Castle. Authorities believed that the crime was committed during the witching hour or the hours darkest before dawn. The newly appointed mayor of Lisbon, Miguel Angel-Angel, thought that only a 'non-believer' could have committed this heinous crime in one of Europe's safest cities. He also mentioned no church services or prayer takes place during those hours, commenting that illicit drugs could be the cause of such an act or the recent migrant epidemic. Drug-related crimes have increased due to the crisis. The entire republic is feeling it. Authorities have not ruled out the African male might of been the victim of a hate crime.

After reading this bit in the paper, Vincent knew *unidentified* meant the man was a vagrant. If the man were thought to be an upstanding member of the community, the mayor and the police would not seem so relaxed in their response to the crime, especially since it was of the uncommon sort in these parts. Another thought (possibly far-fetched?) passed through Vincent's mind—it was Fausto who was the murderer. He noticed his cot was empty the night it happened.

WE'RE ALL
STRANGE + SLUT + PIG EYES

I guess he's okay, Kiki said to Vincent as they sat one evening after dinner.

You spend a lot of time with him, Vincent claimed.

Not really.

Seems like it.

He makes me feel good. He makes me laugh, she said as she wiped her nose with the inside of her hands, swiping upward.

Does he speak of me? Vincent asked.

Not really.

Nothing at all?

I don't think so...he's strange though.

In what way?

Kiki smiled, blushed, her large face turned a deep crimson. Her reaction was a cross between discomfort and satisfaction. It was a peculiar look. She kept digging inside her left ear, the one with the string of earrings. She avoided the question.

In what way? Vincent asked again in a gentler tone.

We're all strange. That's no secret. Her thin lips pursed tight. If you look closely, he has the eyes of a pig.

What a queer thing to say, Vincent thought.

I haven't really noticed.

He does things. I let him. He does other things. Sometimes, it makes me feel good.

Does things? Like?

She felt she had spoken too much, tried to change the subject, her face now returned to her normal color.

I thought you were friends. Don't you talk much? She asked.

Not lately.

He keeps promising things. In return, I let him do things. Things that get him off.

Vincent didn't respond. He sat silent. In fact, he didn't know how to respond. His thoughts about his friend were somewhat mangled, at present.

Kiki continued. He talks about the most delicious foods and drinks. Fancy items for our type. You see, he can get me these things. He has friends around town. He knows grocers, has friends in the pasteleiras, all over. Fausto talks of the most obvious things. He tells me that drinking milk will help your bones not grow weak. He points to his body, how big he is. I know this stuff. I think he tells me these things because I'm large like him. She smiled. I'm not so sure—but I get him.

What does he say about me? Vincent asked again.

Not much. I never ask.

Does he offer you anything?

Huh?

I mean, would he say anything about me without you

asking?

No, mostly he brags about himself. He does all the talking. She let out a brief laugh which sounded like a little squeal. I'm patient. I don't like to talk much.

You're talking a bit now, Vincent said.

Well, you're easy to talk to. Also—you're cute.

Andrea put her hand on Vincent's knee. Her face turned a deep crimson again.

I'm not a slut, she said.

I never thought you were.

I like to be affectionate. You seem sweet.

Uh—thanks.

I'm surprised he hasn't told you.

What?

Fausto. I'm surprised he hasn't bragged about it.

What??

His getting with me. Grabbing on me. She indicated her breasts, her smallish breasts. He touches me a lot. I let him. From the very beginning. I let him try some things.

Why do you let him? What's the point of it??

I look at his dead eyes, his pig eyes, when he gets close. When he gets close to my face. He grunts, puts on an act like he's really turned on.

An act?

Yeah, he's into weird things.

You shouldn't let him.

I didn't.

You should back him off.

I didn't let him.

You didn't?

I didn't. I mean—go all the way.

Vincent realized how odd their conversation was. She

seemed to warm up to him suddenly. There was instant trust on her part—even though this was their first, true conversation. Her advance felt forced. Her hand was no longer on his knee. He heard her wheezing, her large body worked laboriously as they sat there. He wanted to ask her about her tattoos but decided against it. She was a talker. Non-stop, it seemed. She was gargantuan. A gentle giant with a sweet disposition.

My door is always open, she assured Vincent, her hand finding its way back on his knee.

He nodded his head not knowing what else to do or say.

INCAN WARRIORS +
TRANCE + PROPHECIES

A hot towel covered his face to the point of being uncomfortable. The shock of it now lessened as it was slowly pulled off upwards over his forehead. Feeling rejuvenated, his skin tingled. His body felt light, from head to toes. Vincent eyed the tin ceiling, the barber's seat being reclined. The corner television was on a low volume. Nowadays, the black and white dinosaur could serve as a museum piece. There was hardly any talking. The barbers went about their work like leaders of a ceremonial rite. Their faces as angular as Incan warriors, experts with a straight razor, Vincent's lathered face would be shaved to perfection. He knew that one small slip could end in blood—a small nick, a half inch cut—ending with a splattering jugular. He thought of mafioso films. Eyes now shut, he heard the slow scrape of the blade over the lump in his throat, a sound so peculiar, similar to sandpaper smoothing a rough edge.

Vincent fell into a trance. His ears perked up as he

heard the guttural cries of cormorants as they performed a roundabout at Carcavelos, the northern edge of the Tagus, about ten miles from the barber shop. Not seagoing creatures, they realized that what they sought was land since they were prone to stay close to shore.

Scissors in hand, the barber took great care to graze and snip, worked on Vincent's hair, shaping the rebellious strands around his ears—his pride and joy. The snip snip of the scissors sounded like rotating blades or similar to a fan, the up and down, the cutting and snipping, then the stropping of the straight blade, which the barber used to thin out his unruly sideburns. All of this calmed Vincent. He could lay there forever, he thought, levitating on the barber's chair.

What he heard beyond the scraping of blade, what caught his attention, many lights year away, was the remnants of a supernova explosion. Hearing the shock waves from the blast, it echoed thousands of light years to reach him. The sound was similar to rolling thunder along a vast, empty plain.

He imagined himself on that plain, in his dream, which he was dreaming, a mix of black/grey clouds swiftly pass. And he sees himself as he will be in twenty years, a sixty-five-year-old man or thereabouts. A broken, frozen vastness surrounds him. The ground beneath him shook, almost lifting him up but not so much as to separate him from earth to sky. And in this dream he was dreaming, he had the strangest premonition—that he was fated never to find out his buried, true past.

Prophecies, prophecies!!

He screamed at the black sky. Vincent took great care to document that he was slipping from his initial barbershop dream. Exposed on the empty plain, he wanted to step backward into the black and white tiled barbershop, the one where he drifted off and where he used to drift off as a young man, where he happily went with his father—a monthly habit—there to doze and dream as the barber worked his magic.

BALDY + FAMILY PHOTO + IBRAHIM

Vincent paid a visit to the Biblioteca Nacional. He spent time researching the archival database at the central library with no luck. He did the same in the past. Also, with no luck. He searched the name *Ignacio Silva*. Many I. Silva's popped up. He tried various entries—Ignacio Silva (Office of Records), Ignacio Silva (Portuguese Registry), etcetera - he found no leads.

His head spun after a couple of hours at the computer, where he worked slowly, asking others doing their own research or the employees who worked in the research section of the library for help. With puffy, darkish bags under his eyes, he turned in his computer passkey and asked if a certain Ignacio Silva worked in the department. It was a desperate move. The rotund man with a balding head and studious frown said he was unable to give out that type of information.

It's of the utmost importance, said Vincent.

Eu entendo a sua situacao.

You do? You understand?

Sim.

Then why don't you tell me if the man works here?

I can't.

It's a matter of life and death.

Vida e morte? Baldy chuckled as he said it.

Sim. Life and death. *Sim. Sim.* Vincent was losing any patience he possessed.

If it's so important, you should get the police involved. Baldy turned to leave.

Can't you just nod your head up and down if he works here? That's all. Simple. Can you do that for me? *Por favor.*

I cannot. Besides, we do not give out that information to any person who walks off the street and we do not give out that type of information to any homeless who ask such things. There are agencies for that.

Can you get another person to help me?

I cannot.

I see someone in that back room. Can you get her for me?

I cannot.

Let me speak to your supervisor.

I am the supervisor, said Baldy.

Why can't you be helpful?

I have been. Try the Office of Records. I'm sure—

Estupido, I have, I have! Vincent rose to a shout.

The woman in the back room peeked her head out to ask if everything was okay. Others raised their necks above their computers, above the ambient glow, to see what all the fuss was about. They slunk back into the whitish glow of their screens. Everyone except Andres, who sat at the very end of one row.

I will call security if you like, Baldy said.

Filho da puta, Vincent muttered as he walked toward Andres.

What are you doing here, Andres asked, barely above a whisper.

What?

What are you doing—

I can ask the same of you. Vincent pulled an empty chair next to Andres who looked uncomfortable as usual—out of sorts, sullen.

Nada a dizer, Andres said.

Really?

Nada para adicionar, Andres continued.

I see you're your old self, Vincent said. Andres shrugged his shoulders at this.

Don't start about Tristao. Don't start.

Fine. Fine.

Or I'll leave, Andres asserted.

Bem. Bem. Vincent answered, leaning back a bit in his chair, his hands up, conceding a minor victory to Andres. Both men sat in silence, looking at others clicking away on their mouses, their faces showing a look of worry as they followed the little arrow that circled on their screens. After more silence Vincent leaned forward and noticed the image on Andres's computer screen. It looked to be a picture of his family. As he looked closer, they stood on a bridge, all of them huddled and smiling, with his young girl in front, nestled between him and his wife, who was beautiful in her own right. The family looked to be on vacation somewhere. Andres broke the silence.

We were on the Pont au Double. That's Notre Dame Cathedral in the background.

You all seem very happy.

Yes...

What an amazing structure, Vincent commented.

We didn't go inside. Too many tourists for our taste. Instead, we went to eat across the way and stared at it as the sun went down. My wife tried snails for the first time.

Really?

Sim.

Did she like them?

Not really. Andres had a faraway look, a deep longing that all men possess at times. He let out a small laugh which ended in tears. The dish was too unusual for her. She is—was—a simple woman. A wrench of pain contorted his face.

Vincent wanted to ask, *Why do this to yourself? Why torture yourself like this?* But instead, more silence. He wished to say something. It would be an opportune time, his friend needing some comfort. Instead, both men sat motionless, looked into the screens like all others who surrounded them.

I share your pain, Vincent said.

I know.

I don't have a family to speak of.

Eu sei.

So...what else? Vincent asked, changing the subject.

Did you hear about next week?

Next week?

Sim.

What about next week?

The change at the church.

The priest?

Sim.

I've been absent from all the rumors.

Everything will change, Andres said.

I guess you're right.

The priest is a good man.

The one who's leaving?

Of course.

Yes. He plays the piano beautifully.

The piano?

Yes.

How do you know? Andres asked.

The person who sat next to them hushed them, gave them a none-to-pleasant look. Both men ducked their heads, acknowledged their fault. Again, they sat silent, the various coughs and conversations of others now being heard. The fading light of day affected the mood inside—a feeling of supplication—bowed heads, a sudden hush, alms of reprieve.

The computer screen went black. Vincent glanced at Andres without moving his head. Andres didn't move. He seemed a wounded child, still weepy.

Have you seen Lucio? Vincent broke the silence.

No. I haven't seen him much. Why?

He gave me a name. A lead.

Huh?

A guy at the Office of Records or so I'm told.

No, I haven't seen him.

Really?

Sim.

Truly?

Sim. Sim.

I think he's fucking with me.

Lucio?

Yes.

Of course he is.

Yes. Vincent let out an unexpected laugh. It grabbed Baldy's attention. Stern looks all around.

What else? Andres asked.

What else?

What next? Andres rephrased.

I'm stuck. That's why I came here.

You've been here before. You've told me.

Of course. I'm at my wit's end. That's why I wanted to ask you about—

Don't. No. No.

Yes. Yes. What's going on with you? There was a slight pause. Andres! Vincent whispered vehemently.

I told you—

I don't give a fuck! I'm stuck going nowhere. I need you to tell—

Not about Tristao.

Yes.

Or I walk.

Is he behind all the stabbings?

Wha—

The guy in front of the church.

No.

The guy up at Castilho?

The one who was raped? Andres was incredulous.

It's the drugs. I know it's the drugs. The crimes reek of it. Tristao reeks of it!

The crimes?

You know the fuck I'm talking about!

A brief pause. You're really getting paranoid.

Both men came to an abrupt stop. An older woman

walked up to Baldy to complain about the jabbering duo. Baldy leaned his head to one side and shot another stern look at Vincent and nodded to the older woman before he picked up the phone on the counter.

I'm not paranoid, Vincent said.

I came here for a peace of mind, Andres said. And spend time with my family.

So did I.

I'm not bothering anyone.

I know.

Well—Andres shrugged. Nothing had changed about how he handled these moments. His tendency to feel cornered evident once again. Both men then peered at the tall windows. There was a thin purplish line that separated the light and the dark. Night draped on them.

Andres, I like you. You're a good man, Vincent said.

Sim.

I miss our friendship. C'mon, talk to me. Don't be like this.

I know.

Yes?

I know...Andres peeked around a bit, his nerves already frayed. His eyes danced.

What? Vincent pressed.

I know of another stabbing.

What?!

Another stabbing. The papers didn't cover it. The cops—

Before he finished library security came stomping up the marbled flight of stairs. Andres quickly logged out, pushed his seat back in a rush and left his passkey and Vincent in his wake. The sudden bustle prompted most eyes to settle on Vincent. Baldy motioned to the security guard that Vincent was the perpetrator.

Ele!

Vincent turned to look at the shadow line outside the tall windows before he rose from the chair and was escorted out of the library. All eyes turned to vagrant, including Ibrahim, who followed Vincent to the library.

In time, the little man said to himself, in time. I have to be certain.

FACELESS FACES +
SOPRANO'S LAMENT + SAVAGE BLOW

There was always the past to excavate. There was a family to which he belonged. Secrets. Things buried. Certain atrocities. The guilt and the burden, individual or collective. The faceless faces, the nameless names, the anonymous and amongst the anonymous was the killer of the homeless or Ignacio Silva or Vincent's father or his father's father.

He rides and rides on the Green Line from one end of the line to the other. Hours would pass like this. On occasion, the metro police would sweep through the train cars and noticed Vincent who was not one to sleep quietly or soundly and they would shake him awake, his legs fallen asleep and they would kick him out at the next stop. Waiting for his disorientation to pass, the other passengers sighed, shot nasty looks at Vincent, disgusted at the inconvenience and the waiting. All the while, he stumbled out, his legs tingling and numb, horse-collared all the way to street level and given a warning.

He's a vagrant. He looks bad. Smells bad. Look at him. Disgusting. He's bat-shit. Something's not right with him.

He's disheveled. A mess. Vincent has heard it all before. He knows the look, that look of judgement—THIS is what you are—Vincent having no say in the matter.

Now on street level far from the church, Vincent looked out beyond himself, beyond his inner torment and noticed the cold empty street and across the way, an old man walking two small dogs. He was at the far northern edge of the city. His destination was another world entire, the southern tip of Alfama, near the great river.

He had many blocks to walk or risk sneaking into another metro stop, but if caught, there was the risk of a night in a police station cell. Having missed dinner, he could not afford to miss breakfast. Already hungry and weary, his prospects dimmed as he noticed that the usually bustling Ave. de Roma was still as stone. Vincent realized he was the sole inhabitant of the street and for a brief moment he sensed that he could be the next victim of the killer—the one hunting the homeless.

He began to run. Run and stumble. His legs like noodles and not at all like his miraculous ears which heard cosmic events or the soprano's lament in Purcell's *Dido and Aeneas* at the symphony hall some miles away. Yes, he ran, panted and stumbled and only he, the only one on the entire European continent, heard the outrage of the stars— wave after wave of it.

Vincent's lungs gave out and as he came to a stop, he was struck a savage blow to the side of the head.

CAFETERIA + NIBBLE + BAND-AID

There was gauze wrapped tightly around Vincent's head. His hair pushed up above the bandage, he looked similar to a patient from an insane asylum. Kiki, Fausto's new flame, came to pick him up, signed his release papers. Fausto refused to do so, as did the parish priest. He's had enough. Besides, he was packing to leave. His time was up. Vincent complained to Kiki about the pain and the slight ringing in his right ear, the side of the blow.

The doctor told me the sound in your ear would eventually go away, said Kiki.

When?

I don't know—soon, I guess. She fed him soup in the hospital cafeteria. It was a free meal. The ER nurse who cared for him was kind enough to give him a meal voucher. Andrea fed two spoons to him and one for herself. Vincent didn't seem to care. He was glad she was with him. He smiled meekly at her.

How's Fausto? He asked.

Horny as ever. Won't keep his hands off me. Her cheeks turned a bright crimson.

Why don't you say something? Why don't you do

something?

I don't know—I like the attention.

My head is killing me, Vincent said.

The doctor gave you these pills, she held up the plastic bottle to show him. You gotta take them, she stressed.

Okay. A pause as Vincent tried to shield the bright outdoor light which filled the cafeteria. Did they catch him? He asked.

The guy who hit you? Please — you know the answer to that, sweetie.

I figured.

You're not THAT important.

Yeah.

A long pause before Kiki said, I can make you feel better—my door is always open. She pulled her chair uncomfortably close to Vincent's.

Okay...

We can start now. She put her right hand on his crotch and began to grope him under the cafeteria table.

Whoa, wait, wait, wait—

Kiki unzipped his pants. Her face very close to his, her attempt at seduction was ill-opportuned and awkward. Vincent was the opposite of aroused, his penis didn't stir. The one thing that came to mind was Fausto's *pig eyes*. He recalled her saying that.

What type of eyes do I have? He blurted out to her as he shifted in his seat hoping to dislodge her grip.

In fact, her grip tightened. It turned into a vigorous shafting. The large windows and bright light of the cafeteria almost washed both of them out. Barely distinguishable, Kiki didn't care if others saw what took place. She leaned into Vincent, using her gigantic, rolling frame to generate an up-down motion.

Do I have pig eyes? Vincent asked.

Sure. Sure.

Do I? His questions as baffling as the scene beneath the table.

Sure. Whatever.

Determined to get him off right there in the cafeteria at the Hospital Julio de Matos, Kiki's eyes theatrically rolled back, feigned pure delight even though she was the one doing all the work. Her body cranked up and down, her lips reached toward Vincent's neck.

Give me a nibble, she said.

I don't have pig eyes.

Give me—

He leaned further back. Don't tell me I have pig eyes.

She noticed how flat his penis was. She stopped, straightened up, cocked her rectangular head backward, noticed his reticence.

What's with you? What's with the eyes? The weird questions?

You told Fausto he had pig eyes.

What?

You heard me.

I don't know what the fuck you're talking about.

You know.

You must be gay, Kiki stated. Fausto's right.

Fausto's stupid.

No, he plays chess.

That doesn't make someone—

I get everyone off. Everyone. Not YOU.

Calm down.

You are like he says.

I don't care what—

You're an asshole.

Acalme-se, he whispered vehemently as he zipped his pants up.

You're filthy and not in a good way. You smell. And that band-aid looks stupid on you.

It's not a band-aid.

You're gay. Admit it. A pause. Admit it.

Failing an answer, Kiki pushed her chair back. That sudden move along with her huffing and puffing and bright red face, similar to a pissed-off giant, shamed an already ashamed and miserable Vincent.

She stormed off, her hips knocked chairs wayward.

Can I have my pills? He asked.

She turned and threw the bottle, struck him on the head. Others in the cafeteria began to laugh. A few choked on their food, incredulous to what just took place.

DOLPHINS +
NEW PRIEST + PATTER OF FEET

No sign of Lucio. No sign of Tristao. He asked around. No one said anything. All became tight-lipped. He felt a pariah. Was Fausto turning people against him? He wished to approach Kiki but decided against climbing that mountain. Feeling lethargic and relaxed, the oxycodone helped Vincent swim with the dolphins off Ponta Delgada. He loved the sea. He loved water. He wasn't meant to be landlocked.

A declaration was made. In two days a new priest from Porto will lead the church. Gossip spread like wildfire throughout the ranks of the homeless. There was the usual drama, the excitable chit chat, talk that the new head priest was of the older generation, a disciplinarian. It would be a work for shelter and food system. Nothing would be guaranteed. Eventually—a first-come, first-served system would be installed—as bureaucratic as everything else, as stale and lifeless as the various agencies that couldn't help Vincent.

Vincent's ear still rung. It affected his previous magic, turned him into a mere mortal. Without it, he felt useless.

For it was in the tiny space between words, the quiet sigh before an aria, the rapid breathing before lovemaking, the wingbeat of the gazelle's flight or the soft patter of an infant's feet. It was his connection to the world. He longed for its return as he longed for some painkiller.

FATHER GABRIELO:
A FEW WORDS

I am here to tell you that there will be change. I come from Porto where I served under Bishop Horacio Cabral for many years. I sought greener pastures. That is why I am here with you today. I look at you, a great many of you, and see deep wounds, hopes dashed, your lease on life tested on a daily basis.

Fear not, for I am with you, be not dismayed, for I am your God; I will strengthen you, I will help you, I will uphold you with my victorious right hand.—Isaiah 41:10

As a man of faith I see little faith in this flock. You have lost your way. We shall regain it. We shall rise again. You will work for it. You will earn your time here. We have been lax. This church has been lax. This will strengthen your resolve and you must prove your faith with your response to the call of the Gospel.

We have heard the news. There is a hunter out there preying on the weak and unfortunate.

Do not be overcome by evil but overcome evil with good.—Romans 12:21

The gossip is that there is a killer amongst us. He

might be sitting next to you. He breathes malice. There is no salvation for this man. He has not chosen God.

Ele respira malicia.

So we look deep into our hearts for in each one of us pulses the divine blood. We are all creatures of God. We seek His counsel. There is much avarice and hate, opportunists and whoremongers. It is easy to lose one's way. In our vice lies our weakness.

Fraqueza.

It is a difficult time in Portugal. We have been hit hard by this crisis. More and more are impoverished. More and more run toward the fire.

Medidas desesperadas.

The divine light has been snuffed out. So we resort to murderous acts. We do not heed the word of God. We run toward the fire. So, I implore you—a challenge if you will—to keep your head down and work hard. You will work. We will work. *Nao mais apatia.*

NAO MAIS APATIA.

We will all keep our eyes and ears open. We will be vigilant. We will heed the word of God. I call on my Lord in my distress and He answers me.

A NOTE

As he was going to bed one night, Vincent found a note placed on his pillow. It read—*Nos estamos observando voce.*

We are watching you.

WHISPERS +
SAD AND LOONY + LIGHT OF TRUTH

Between regular visits to the library and scrubbing the floors or doing some odd job in the church, Vincent was in the hunt for painkillers. He walked around either numb or high most of the time. In between the two extremes came the pain.

He had trouble focusing on anything in particular. His recent hallucinations included photographs from recent books, recurring motifs, a certain line he read from a passage or poem which he repeated constantly, quietly to himself.

We are watching you.

Inexplicably, Vincent became drawn to the terrible images of Auschwitz, Belzec and Treblinka. How were such crimes possible? Is this the result of human endeavor? What sickness or mania allowed for such things? An entire nation hoodwinked by a maniac—an art school flunky no less!

We are watching you.

Pain tormented him. Images of pestilence, disfigured corpses, piles of skeletal bodies—all whispered to Vincent.

These whispers grew the more he returned to the images in the books. Is this what the others hear? Is this the madness that imprisons most of the homeless? Was he now one of the sad and loony who wander and blabber about?

He walked back and forth from one side of Lisbon to the other. East to west, west to east. Hounded by something besides the pain, possibly the images of death, images that he couldn't fathom. Vincent sensed some odd association with all of it. He couldn't put it into words but he felt it in his bones.

A name resurfaced—Ignacio Silva. Would this man be able to help? Prevent Vincent from falling into total oblivion?

Vincent wished to renew his search for Silva but there was the pain and his need to curb it. Painkillers. He would seek Andres. He had to. He could put Vincent in touch with the street pharmacopeia that could help snuff out the searing light that tormented him. But then, there was the light of truth that Vincent would eventually have to deal with.

PIMP + NATIVES RESTLESS + WOLVES

Vincent woke to see Fausto seated in the cot next to his. He was sipping from a bottle of Coca-Cola, a straw in the corner of his mouth. Vincent rose with great effort, groggy from the Codeine he took a couple hours prior.

What do you want?

You're an asshole, Fausto responded.

You're a bigger one.

You want a sip? He offered Vincent the remains of his soda.

Nao.

Fausto shrugged his shoulders and looked down, his eyes crisscrossed as he siphoned off the rest of his drink.

What do you want? Vincent asked again.

I have a favor to ask.

No favors. Go fuck yourself.

I'll make it worth your while.

Leave me alone, I'm tired as hell.

As Vincent began to slip back down on the cot, Fausto leaned forward.

Everything will be forgiven if you do this for me.

Stop playing games.

Do me this one thing.

What do you want?

Help me hurt the guy at the shop.

What? The what??

The grocer. You know who I'm speaking of.

The grocer?

Don't act dumb. Help me do this.

No.

Help me.

No.

Help me do this and I put the past behind us. We start with a clean slate. A slight pause. I'll let you fuck Kiki, Fausto added.

What are you, her pimp?

You know how it works.

Huh?

Don't ask stupid questions.

Mae de Deus.

We go after him. Hurt him. Make him stop what he's doing.

Doing? What's he doing?

I don't want to go into details.

Well...

Why make me say it.

Forget it.

He roughs up Kiki. He fucks her, roughs her up. Makes me watch. He's a nasty prick.

Shush!

Those close by grew tired of the banter. Both men glanced about. There was a full moon. A good deal of it spilled into the large hall. The two men were tired, the dark of their eyes the size of large grapes. Fausto's hair grew back. He saw the big man rub his elbow, his bursitis acting up.

You keep asking me to do your dirty work, Vincent whispered.

Dirty work?

Sim. Last time it was Tristao.

Don't be a hypocrite.

A bit of silence as Fausto dabbed a handkerchief on his forehead a few times.

I've heard nothing from Tristao, Vincent claimed.

He's around.

You've seen him?

Fausto nodded. He glanced round again, his face took on a phosphorous glow. He was in obvious pain thanks to his elbow.

Where is he, then? Vincent asked.

Tristao?

Sim.

He has in hand in everything. He has young girls working for him.

Young girls?

Teens. Around that age. He pimps them out.

You're kidding.

Drugs are involved.

I'm sure. A slight pause. How's Andres involved?

I don't know. I don't keep tabs on him.

Another *shush!!* Followed by a *bichano!!*

The natives are getting restless.

Well?

Vincent took a moment—No, count me out.

This is the only time I'll ask, was Fausto's ultimatum.

Vincent shrugged and slid back into the cot. Fausto

rose to his feet.

Before he stepped away, Vincent reached over and took out a slip of paper from his suitcase.

Did you do this? He handed the note to Fausto.

Fausto read the words *We are watching you* to himself.

I don't play games, he said and handed it back.

Did you?

That's not my handwriting. You made the wrong move by not helping me.

The Fausto that Vincent knew a few months back was not the threatening type. He saw his large figure fade into the shadows. With half-closed eyes, he noticed that his one-time friend had a limp about him as well.

The fat man was dealing with his own wounds, he thought. Before he put his head to his pillow, Vincent counted sheep amidst all the wolves.

MUSEUM + MAN
IN WINDOW + YOU DON'T BELONG

Vincent walked west on Rua Dom Luis to Largo Santos and then onto Calcada Ribeiro Santos. He turned south and there was the wide expanse of the Rio Tajo. On these walks he was oblivious to distance or distance covered. Restless, he walked to take his mind off certain things, to run away from the pain, to distract himself. The hygiene he was once so proud of was no longer evident. He let himself go to hell. It became an inconvenience. His smell was offensive, more so if you traveled in his wake.

He passed the same shops. One shop blurred into another. On occasion, he would end up in a spot in which he had no idea how he got there, so scattered were his thoughts, so strong his pain.

One of these surprises came when he found himself in front of the steps of the National Museum of Antique Art—an area which became a new roaming ground for Vincent—east of the Alcantara district. It was not nearly as crowded or hectic as the Alfama. He enjoyed the quiet and slower pace of this *bairro*. And being the tail end of the cold season, there was very little stirring on these streets.

We are watching you.

Standing on the steps just outside the main entrance on Rua das Janelas Verdes, he looked in both directions, east and west. Nary a soul. He looked again, his gaze lingered, he studied the near and far horizon and still—no one. There were pigeons, a cat crossing the street, a plastic bag swirled round. He peered at the buildings across the street. He scanned the facades and stared intently at each building, all windows so largely elongated, Vincent noticed. Again, no human presence.

Vincent looked at his feet, rubbed his aching neck, felt unusually thirsty, scratched the bridge of his nose and looked back up to see a man who stood behind one of the large windows directly across from him. He was on the third floor, his hands pressed flat against the glass, completely naked. Behind him was a man who looked to be in a black uniform, a red Nazi armband clearly visible. The man in uniform, with pomaded hair, pants dropped to his ankles, was fucking the man whose hands were pressed against the windows. Both men's eyes zeroed in on Vincent. The man who was being penetrated was completely covered, head to toe, in a white powdery substance.

Startled, Vincent tripped on the step behind him. As he fell, his body twisted halfway round. He braced his fall with his forearms on the edge of the next flight of steps, he went down so quickly. A shot of pain jolted through his body. The pain in his head did the same. Everything screamed.

From his vantage point, sprawled slantwise, he had a direct line of sight to the window. They were no longer there. Actually, Vincent couldn't be certain, the glare being so strong from this particular angle. What was certain was the look of malice and hate directed at him before his fall.

After a quick glance over his shoulder, Vincent rose and scuttled into the museum. Without thinking, he took a flight of steps to his right. No one seemed to notice. He hobbled up the steps, gathered himself in a corner two floors up. His forearms and head burst with pain. Shafts of sunlight brightened the stairwell. Vincent breathed heavily. He continued one flight up and slipped into the main building where the exhibits were held. Not many people were around. He saw an older couple at the other end of the hallway. They had the look of tourists but there was no one else.

He walked carefully, still hurting badly from the fall. Paranoid and anxious, wary of not belonging, Vincent didn't want to bring attention to himself, even though his general appearance was no help. He found himself in a small, quiet room with faded yellow walls. There was one painting—a triptych—in the room. At first glance he didn't think much of it. After a stronger look, he was pulled forward.

What Vincent saw shocked him. He scanned the three-paneled artwork from left to right. He scanned it slowly since there was so much to see, so much detail. It was unlike anything he had ever seen. Most of the figures were indescribable. It was part surreal, part horror, part macabre, utterly religious—the overall vision of the work—nightmarish.

At the top of the left panel was the figure of a monk flying on the back of some ghoulish figures. Upon closer inspection, there was a ghoul with his backside sticking up in the air—a motif in the painting—for there was another huge ass sticking up in the middle of the left panel beneath a mound of earth. There was a mixture of human figures and not so human figures—disfigured souls, midgets, strange creatures—all vying for attention.

The middle panel was the largest and demanded the most attention. His eyes were drawn to the large fire, a massive inferno that consumed a village in the background. Leaning closer, he saw tiny figures on horses, skeletons on the back of a large flying fish and in the foreground more of the same. Birds and various winged creatures populated the work. There were some pious figures, one of them at the very center peering over his shoulder directly at those who looked at the painting. There was another on the far right panel doing the same, he was holding a bible, only to reveal that he was blind.

Here was this horrific excess, fantastical and hard to imagine, something he just stumbled upon. He could not tear himself away. The more time passed, the more he looked, his eyes peeled from one image to the next.

Two museum guards walked into the room. One of them said, *Voce nao pertence aqui.*

The other gestured the way out. Both men repulsed by Vincent's smell, they led him to the same place he entered, onto Rua das Janelas Verdes. As he was shoved onto the street, Vincent sheepishly glanced at the building across the street, the same as before. There was no one to be seen. In fact, it seemed as if he entered the museum an entire day earlier. Gone was the sunshine and bright glare. Instead, the typical grey clouds—low, fast, ominous.

FATHER GABRIELO:
LET US NOT BE UNGRATEFUL

I am beginning to see tents sprout up all over the city. Is this the sign of the times? Is this what we have become? It is painfully obvious we have abandoned these people. We are all God's children—are we not? Shelter, food, health, safety—all of these comforts should be granted to us. But some say life is unfair and that is the way it is. It is a cynical perspective and we live in a cynical age. I say no. NO. I refuse to believe this. I say the word of God is what matters. His covenant is our protector. HE is our shelter and not these tents—these makeshift homes. So we live in shadows, under bridges, in empty canals, alleys of all sorts. Refugees, mainly. But what is the true meaning of refugee?

(A very long silence.)

They are not meant to be seen. That is what I think. They are not meant to be seen. But we are all refugees of some sort, are we not? And God has given us shelter. God has not forgotten us. *The meek shall inherit the Earth.* He has blessed us. We are the inheritors. Let us not be ungrateful.

BERSERK + CUCKOLD + RAPE

Fausto was seen walking with a cane, limping heavily. Kiki was crying, wiped her tears with both hands. Around them was their usual group. Fausto gave a single, long look to Vincent. It was an accusatory look as if what happened was Vincent's doing.

See what you have caused.

From what he could gather, it seemed that Fausto stood up to the grocer. The grocer went berserk, frothed at the mouth, became indignant. Fausto knew the deal, you cannot break what was established, 'You're ripping me off!' and other accusations—all the while pounding Fausto with his fists. Kiki pointed to the bruises on the back of his neck. One person from the group shook her head in disbelief, another almost laughed. Kiki paid no attention and kept up her frantic monologue.

The grocer groped her aggressively, forced his tongue in her mouth. He then thrust his hand down her pants, all the while making the cuckold (Fausto)—watch. He screamed he would only fuck Kiki from now on, that he wouldn't touch him. (She let the cat out of the bag). The big woman then said Fausto stood up for her. He pushed the grocer from behind, even though he bled from the mouth and his head was like soft fruit. The grocer became enraged and grabbed a broom. He hit Fausto repeatedly, injuring his right knee. She then said that after he beat Fausto into submission, he tied him up, poured olive oil and flour on him, slapped him around some more and then—

She glanced at Fausto who grimaced in pain and still stood, possibly trying to prove that he could take any beating and still stand. Fausto gestured to her, tried to make her quit talking. She ignored him. She told her captive audience that the grocer raped her.

Ele me estuprou! Ele me estuprou!!

The cuckold had been cuckolded. Fausto stood, teetered on his cane, unable to look anyone in the eyes.

KELP FOREST +
SANSKRIT + NOT SOUND

Normally at this time of night, Vincent could hear the gigantic cargo ships make their way out to sea or the various barges spear up and down the Tagus, their wakes rippling to shore. These sounds could easily wake him before the blow to his head. Now, he was like most of the other tramps, snoozing away. He took two painkillers right before bed to ensure a sound sleep.

Pigeons fluttered about. Nothing was out of the ordinary. A variety of wheezes and snores broke the quiet. Vincent laid in bed, flat on his back, arms at his sides. An unusual position from him but the painkillers did their work. He had a reflective look on his face. It was possible he dreamt of something or somewhere far away. The expression on his face near curiosity as if he were searching for something. Seals. He wished for seals.

His dreaming mind then thought of some underwater kelp forest. Shafts of sunlight dissolved into the dark beneath him. Sanskrit scrawl now appeared below Vincent's feet which scissor-kicked like some underwater ballet dancer. The Sanskrit letters faded in and out, some words served as various clues that only he could comprehend. They were bad omens. Terrible omens having to do with crimes against humanity. And then it came, the teeth—his bad teeth—fell out. Then, without warning, his eyes popped open.

Vincent woke to find his mouth gagged and his body roped to his cot. What came next was a few vicious punches to his midsection. He screamed in pain but the gag forced the sound back into him. The punches, swift and brutal, found his ribcage and worked their way down to his crotch where the final blow fell. And just like that the ropes slackened and the assault ended.

He turned on his side, folded over and took the cot with him to the tiled floor. With a thud, his body contorted, this way and that. He wanted to scream. The gag left in his mouth still blocked any sound from escaping. Coughing, then whimpering, he curled up, writhed some more until the night and the absolute silence swallowed him till any sound coming from him wasn't even sound.

SNUFFED OUT +
CIRCUS ACT + LAST WORDS

I heard what happened to you, said Kiki.

Vincent didn't respond. Just silence. He twirled his Chinese bracelet, thought of the Haitian.

You don't seem like yourself.

What is that supposed to mean?

The life in your eyes. Snuffed out.

Que merda?!

Kiki laughed. A pitying laugh. Yep, what the fuck, is right. Like, what the fuck happened to you?

What do you care? A slight pause. Leave me alone.

Vincent wished to leave but he was in too much pain. Everything aggravated him. Kiki was no help. He tried to avoid the beast.

Aren't you going to ask me—

What?

Who did that to you? The people who hurt you.

Feche e boca.

Another laugh. She looked down at him. She didn't attempt to sit on the empty cot next to his. Vincent looked unbelievably small next to her. She could be a major act in a circus, he thought.

Go back to your pimp, said Vincent. Leave me the hell alone.

That's funny. You're funny. Sooo funny. I'm taken care of. Do you see me suffering? Like you? I'm well taken care of.

You already said that.

You're stupid.

How 'bout Fausto?

Silence as she tried to avoid his searching look. She looked down at her enormous feet.

What about Fausto? He asked again.

He's useless.

Wow—just like that?

That's how it goes.

Wow.

Guys like you and him don't last, she claimed.

Paulo came by mopping the floor. Aptly named, he was short in height. Kiki eyed him in that way of hers. Her eyes unclothed the scrawny fellow—the man whose name meant *Little One*. Intent on doing his work he averted her lusty stare as best he could, the tip of his tongue pressed out the corner of his mouth.

I don't know anyway, Kiki broke the silence.

What don't you know?

Who beat the shit out of you.

Right.

I wouldn't tell you anyway.

Your big secret?

Another pause. The pigeons became worked up.

You're still a dick. I eat well. I get fucked all the time. What do you do? You sit here like a loser who gets tossed around, beaten to shit. And you better leave while you have the chance.

Those were the last words Kiki ever spoke to Vincent.

IBRAHIM + LIFE'S WORK + BIG SECRET

Vincent met a man from Tel Aviv. A very small, thin man. Probably in his late seventies, he spoke in a hush and boasted that he spoke a few languages. Just arrived in Portugal. I used to be a lawyer, he said. He had a pulpy nose, blue/green eyes, fair complexion, a good number of moles. He just walked up to Vincent and started to speak to him. Vincent had to lean in, almost knocking both of them over. His name was Ibrahim. A gypsy, he professed. A Jew, nonetheless. He pointed to his nose. Vincent laughed. Someone with a sense of humor. Self-deprecating, but it was a relief. They stood near the entrance to the library.

Vincent would get the shivers lately. Ibrahim asked if he was well. Vincent deflected his question and spoke about his name.

Ibrahim sounds Arabic.

It is.

You don't look anything like an Arab.

My mother named me. My father was the Jew. She was Mizrahim.

Mizrahim? Vincent asked.

Arab-speaking Jew.

Ah.

Not everyone is a dead giveaway.

Vincent looked at the leather attache bag Ibrahim was holding. It was extremely worn down.

My life's work, he said.

Oh.

Both men took a break to look at the people passing in and out of the doors. Vincent buttoned up as if it would lessen his shivering. It didn't. Vincent continued his inquiry.

What is it you do?

I'm retired from my law practice. I've a new passion.

Oh.

Yes, it keeps me occupied. It requires research and patience. This is my research, Ibrahim pointed to his bag. He clutched it tight, Vincent noticed.

Vincent enjoyed the dark of the library. His head didn't pound as much, his eyes didn't squint as much, his breathing eased. Vincent kept probing.

What type of research?

Oh, I'm not inclined to say.

A big secret?

Not as exciting as that, I'm afraid. I find it difficult in my advanced age.

The research?

Finishing what I set out to do, the little man said with exactitude.

Silence. The old man continued.

As one gets older, priorities shift. My wife died thirteen years ago. She was from Manitoba—the Lakes region. Do you know what I'm referring to?

No, I'm not familiar—

There's a vastness to where she's from. One can get lost among the numerous lakes or forests. Stretches as far as one can see.

Sounds beautiful. Does such a place still exist?

Ibrahim didn't answer. He instead asked Vincent if he visited the library regularly.

Yes, I do. It's one of—

Well, I shall see you around. Ibrahim interrupted as if he already knew the answer.

Vincent barely heard him. He shuffled away giving one long last look to Vincent—uncomfortably long, with an edge to it. Ibrahim walked out the doors with his slightly stooped gait, his right hand still coiled around his leather case.

IN LOVE + MAN JUMPS + RAW COLD

Needing fresh air Vincent stepped out of the church. The smell of the sea was strong. It's as if he had not experienced it in years. The recent events so strange, even his prior life and troubles seemed halfway normal. He found himself indoors more often. Part of it was the new rules preventing late night carousing. Lisbon was usually a ghost town during the winter months—more so with all of the new rules.

The fresh air cleared a space in his head. The static thoughts took a rest. At that moment, he wished to be in love. There was a lonely place in his heart. He was partial to this feeling. He felt time was running out. In better days he would sometimes fantasize of a woman in the same predicament, whom he would mentor, who would cherish him and his knowledge, his love of names and what they meant, the power of his creative mind, how kind he was. He knew things. He could care for another. He could prove that.

Vincent looked eastward to his right and there was a large figure of a man who resembled Fausto. He was some distance away and Vincent couldn't really tell if in fact it was the big man. He looked to be holding a cane. He squinted his eyes, hoped that would bring this man into focus.

The man looked to be on the verge of jumping over the wall if he could raise his giant body to do so. He would need the help of his cane. Vincent stood, petrified. He wished to edge closer to get a better look but sensed the slightest movement would bring attention to himself and cause the man to actually jump.

The man seemed near death—his look, his gait, his overall mood. Vincent wished to make a move but his entire body betrayed him. He began to pant, looked round to see if others were near. No, only him and this potential jumper. Vincent whirled round, caught in some terrible momentum he couldn't control. The world spun, then tilted. All motion came to an abrupt stop. His panting increased, he noticed the tingle in his fingertips. He turned back in the direction of the Fausto look-alike and saw nothing. He turned the other direction, certain he was facing the wrong way and nothing.

Did he jump??

And still, Vincent couldn't move. It was as if he were in some nightmare, his feet and legs not obeying what his brain told him. He became desperate. Did the man jump?! His two hands grabbed his right leg, attempted to unearth it, move it forward, all the while grunting and spewing profanity. He tried the same with his other leg, sinking deeper into the imbroglio he found himself. Exhausted with his labors, he fell to the ground, his knees almost shatter from the fall.

Night came. Raw cold. He peeled himself from the stone tiles. His pants scuffed at the knees, pangs of hunger stirred. He heard the church bells and realized he missed dinner and curfew. He would be locked out. If he attempted entry—he would be punished further—Gabrielo would deny him further lodging. Vincent would have to tough it out till morning, keep one eye open.

MORGUE + MILKY WHITE + SICK JOKE

The man did jump to his death. Vincent missed the tragic moment as he himself collapsed. It was all a whirl. He sat dejected as the police questioned him. He agreed to identify the body, thinking it was Fausto. Gabrielo refused to look at the corpse. The padre's already skewed sense of morality baffled even the police and those investigating the motives of the suicide.

Vincent felt like jumping himself as he stood in the morgue where the dead man's body lay. The smell of antiseptic was strong, nauseating. He stood there repelled by the bloated figure on the steel table, half-determined to identify his former friend, if in fact it was Fausto.

Distracted by his cell phone, the investigator stood off to the side, patiently waiting for Vincent, who took another step closer toward the body. As he looked, he was first drawn to the man's very large figure. The girth of his waistline was similar to Fausto's. His one-time friend didn't possess the shoes that were removed and placed by his feet or even the belt that was of the same nice leather. These items belonged to a man of some wealth or so it seemed. The shirt was a designer shirt, something that could be purchased at one of the fancy shops on Rua Aurea.

Vincent stepped even closer, the man's face obscured by the size of his body. What he saw shocked him. Partially disfigured, he was not certain this was his friend's face. The skin was milky white—absurdly so. The veins, the color of red or some deep purple, were very noticeable. The stark white of the man's face overwhelmed all else. For a moment, Vincent flinched thinking the man's lips quivered. True, there was no distinct feature that made him think that this was Fausto. The dead man's hair, beautifully combed back, made it all seem like some sick joke.

Vincent turned round, the investigator was still buried deep in his cell phone, doing his best of going through the motions. Looking back at the slab of flesh, the face at once hideous and mesmerizing—a gamut of feelings played out. For a brief second, he was certain this was Fausto. He then recalled the tattoo that that his friend got inked on his forearm. He tried to recall the words as the investigator began to tap his foot, his patience thinning.

Can you please roll up his sleeves? Vincent asked.

Que?

My friend has a—

I can't do that. Against the rules.

My friend has a mark on—

Que? The investigator took a strong step toward Vincent.

A tattoo. Vincent indicated his forearms.

Tattoo?

Sim.

I just said we can't touch the body. What part of that—

He has a tattoo on his forearm, then I can be certain.

You don't call the shots, *minha amiga.*

Of course, I realize—

I already told you—

Please.

Nao. Nao mais. He made a gesture swiping his hand across his neck.

Por favor! Vincent implored.

The investigator flipped his cell phone shut and slipped it into his jacket pocket. He stood and contemplated the next move. He quickly brushed past the vagrant and began to unbutton the dead man's cufflinks. He then stopped. Vincent began to retch, the smell getting to him.

Now bent over—Vincent took a few, slow breaths.

You need some fresh air? the investigator asked.

No—I don't think so.

He stayed bent over. He thought of Fausto. He thought of the first time he saw him, feeding pigeons in Praca Comercio. Showered bread crumbs, a king and his minions, as content as a man could be.

No tattoos, the investigator said as he patted Vincent on his back.

Vincent slowly curled upright. He had to steady himself, his knees uncertain, the sight of the corpse still unsettling.

Now do you believe me? The investigator continued.

Vincent focused in on the dead man's forearms. True to the man's word, he didn't see a tattoo. He recalled the words on Fausto's forearm—*Plus de poids.*

We need to wrap up here, the investigator said. Have you seen what you needed to see?

One moment, Vincent said.

He stepped forward, still uncertain—the recycled air of the morgue as lifeless as the dead body. Sure enough, there was no tattoo on either forearm. He gazed for some moments, only to keep looking. The closer he looked, he could faintly make out a smudge of what looked to be a previous tattoo on the right forearm with the letter P most visible. So he leaned closer and before he could be certain, the investigator pulled down both sleeves.

It's time to go, he ordered.

I didn't really get a chance to—

Doesn't matter. I'm not getting screwed over because of you. Let's go.

I need more time, Vincent pleaded.

No way. He reached for his cell phone and began to dial the police station.

Well—is this your friend or not?

FATHER GABRIELO:
ANOTHER SERMON

I will share with you a passage from Psalms—*Blessed are those who do not walk in step with the wicked or stand in the way that sinners take or sit in the company of mockers.* Here, in Lisbon, as in all of Portugal, we are struggling. A crisis has hit our country. Many are impoverished, desperate. A man throws himself off a ledge. There are people attacking each other in the street. Crime is beginning to manifest itself. Our food supplies seem to be at risk with an upcoming transportation strike. Our railways operate at half capacity. Tourists stay away. Need I go on?

There were happier times. There will be happier times. I recall a time as a young man—if you allow me to reminisce—I traveled to Paris. It was my first time out of Portugal, me and a group of fellow seminary students. As you know, I'm from Porto, a northerner. We are not as worldly as you southerners. So you can imagine Paris was like sliding down the rabbit hole. What did I see? Of course there was the famous river, The Seine. I have walked along its banks. I have stood on the various bridges, made famous by their movies and books, where I saw fishermen, couples in love, the tiny book stalls and as I continued walking, east along this river. I passed the cathedral of Notre Dame. I had to see with my own eyes what everyone speaks of. And maybe it was the time of day but I stood transfixed. I became caught up with the sight of this magnificent building. The sky looked like the color of salmon, Paris at dusk. And in this unique light basked the cathedral.

As we continued our eastward trek, along the quays, beneath the Pont de Sully, a bridge that connected to the Ile Saint-Louis—there were more treasures! We found out the history of the monks and the Knights Templar who established themselves on the right bank—the city being divided by the right and left bank—depending on what side of the river you rest. Many of these men were burned at the stake, the leaders of the time paranoid about their influence.

And yet, their history, the same stones and pavements on which we walked, the numerous buildings, churches, monuments—was drenched in some form of prior calamity. The history that we read, that one person or another—our guide, the locals, plaques commemorating some important event—was steeped in blood, death or sacrifice. Joan of Arc, most of you have heard the name, was tried and burned at the stake. Boccaccio, the Florentine poet, described in his famous book the same fate for the Knights Templar, whose screams can still be heard today.

So on my subsequent walks, I reflected on all of this history, one could not escape it. At times, I felt as if I were walking suspended, as if on air, becalmed. I could breathe easily and freely, always with a lifted feeling and I was certain my face showed a certain peaceful look. My thoughts lay scattered. The abundance with Parisian life, the joy of life that seems so common to the French way, in direct contrast to those who paid the price. It was not lost on me that my thoughts lay like a heavy crown upon my head. I was beset with anxiety during this period. A pestilence ravaged me—my own past, my very own sins, my studies at seminary. Paris lifted these worries for a time. I tell you I could breathe again, freely and openly. My lungs filled with hope. My heart felt this too. I was happy.

In closing, I share a passage from Isaiah—*All of us have become like one who is unclean, and all our righteous acts are like filthy rags; we all shrivel up like a leaf, and like the wind our sins sweep us away.*

ANOTHER NOTE

We'll gut you like a fish. Another note Vincent found on his pillow.

ANOTHER VICTIM +
KILLING GROUND + SOMETHING BAD

Another victim was found. Another homeless male. Half the victim's face was partially disfigured, his skull caved in. Once again, the pants were coiled around the victim's ankles, his backside exposed to the morning light. He was found face down, arms at his sides, like the previous cases. The victim's palms faced upwards, warmed by Lisbon's springtime sun. The posture, at once disturbing, also expressed a soul at rest. The crime looked to be some type of sacrifice.

This was the second victim to be found at Julio de Castilho, a stone's throw from the church. The popular tourist spot turned into a killing ground. This particular soul was none other than Andres Arnaldo Cabral or *Andres* as he was known to Vincent.

Maybe the crimes were a message not only one person was sending but many? Possibly the government or possibly a faction that worked hand in hand with the police—since nothing seemed to be done about any of this.

Poor Andres, he thought. How did this happen? Was Tristao involved? Is he still a threat? Tristao had a larger presence in the underworld with his drug and sex trafficking and could have been a supplier of Vincent's very own pills. Tristao had friends. He had his enemies. Vincent hadn't set eyes on him in months but still sensed his presence.

The Portuguese went about their business and their simple concerns regardless of what happened. Radicalism was spreading. Spain was a victim of attacks. Germany. England. In France, it as almost certain there would be attacks of some kind or other.

We'll gut you like a fish.

Would Vincent make it through the evening? Would he indeed be gutted? His throat slashed? His head caved in like Andres'? Was he on some list? Was someone watching? Waiting? His intuition told him that something bad will happen.

RETURN TO ESTRELA +
MORE FAUSTO + CLOUDBURST

It was a Sunday. Vincent found himself in Jardim da Estrela. Weeks passed since he had ventured this far. The winter months were eventful. No more Lucio, Tristao, Andres, Fausto, Kiki was nowhere to be seen. Last Vincent heard she was the grocer's sex toy, sex slave, what have you. Andres' murder weighed on Vincent. He walked around as he normally did when he was in the park, very careful not to bring attention to himself. There was a slight chill in the air. His voice shook as he spoke to himself.

He was not in as much pain. Maybe the cold and damp of the past months worsened it. And as he calmly strolled, tiny steps, here and there in the park, always returning to his favorite spot—he could not help think of Fausto's blanched body, bloated and veiny, floating down the Tagus and eventually out to sea. This was the dream he's been having. It consumed him at times—the image of his lifeless slab on a frigid, metallic table. So final and absolute.

Vincent glanced in the direction of one of the ponds. Skirting the pond were peacocks, a common sight. Almost trampling the birds were some teens on skateboards, faces buried in phones, blind to the commotion they caused.

Filhos da puta! Ha ha ha! Bichano!

No one took offense to the garbage they spewed. Actually, one mother pushing a stroller showed a hint of emotion but not enough to prove she cared. All of Portugal didn't seem to care. That was the issue—the apathy of the country. The lack of anything getting done, being done, about anything and everything. And still, Vincent couldn't rid his mind of the image of his friend's pulpy carcass being sucked out to sea.

And it began to rain. How could it? It was a cloudless sky except for a single cloud that looked more like a brown smudge.

The cloudburst turned into a fine mist. And through the spray Vincent noticed Fryda. He hadn't seen the queen of the metro in months. She had now emerged away from her usual spots between the Baixa and Martim Moniz stations. He noticed that her dog was not at her side. Also absent were the gaggle of homeless who usually sought her counsel.

She sat, her knees pressed together, hands on her knees, as still and contemplative as the young priests at Santa Lucia. As he continued walked toward her in his careful way, a large airliner streaked over the park, lower than usual, causing the numerous pigeon, the peacocks and children to scatter and scream about. The flight path to Portela Airport flew directly above Jardim da Estrela. It made Vincent's hair stand on end. It was so close he could clearly see the TAP on the tailfin.

As the ground shook, Fryda just sat there. She looked to be in a trance. Vincent eventually approached her, the rain now passed. *Boa tarde*, Fryda.

GREEN TOENAILS +
BONSAI + STARE AT DUCKS

Fryda glanced up, the sun directly in her eyes. She saw Vincent's silhouette, his head now eclipsed the sunlight. There was an uneasiness about her, much different than her usual disposition. Agitated, she spoke.

What do you want?

It's Vincent.

Leave me be, she waved him off with a gesture.

Where's Gertrude?

She didn't respond. Glumly, she shifted on the bench.

Your dog? A stretch of silence. Fryda?

More silence. Her eyes looked toward her feet. She wore sandals. Her toes curled. Vincent was at a loss. Perplexed by her mood, he stepped aside and her body was now blanched in light. Vincent turned his head around, looked about, noticed a return to normalcy after the plane roared by.

May I sit, he asked?

She shrugged her shoulders. Barely a shrug at all.

He sat, eased into the slight curve in the bench. He let out a sigh. His feet were sore.

I wish I had tobacco. I could really enjoy a smoke right now. Times have been tough. A pause. Rough winter, don't you think?

Fryda began humming to herself. Eyes still downcast. Vincent looked at her toes. Her toenails were painted green.

Vincent couldn't tell if her silence was conscious or not. Was this the silent treatment or was her mind out to pasture? He couldn't decide.

Fryda, where's your dog?

She died. Fryda finally said. Struck by a car. It happened a couple months ago. It was cold out. It was such a lousy day that we—

A swift breeze blew through the park, caused ripples in the various ponds. Spray from the fountains also blew toward the direction of the Basilica. Children laughed. Dogs barked. Birds shambled in all directions. Vincent spoke.

I'm very sorry to hear—

It was outside Martim Moniz, crossing Rua Fernandes da Fonseca. I became tangled up with my shopping cart, accidentally let go of her leash. The cart tipped over. It was a—mess.

Vincent wanted to say something but decided against it. So both of them sat there awkwardly. Vincent craved a smoke. Fryda yearned for something else, something improbable (like most things).

As both of them looked straight ahead, Fausto reappeared in Vincent's mind. He was walking jovially to the kiosk near Vincent's favorite tree. He asked for a Coke. He made a comment or two. Tourists were aghast at some sexual innuendo he made. They muttered that tramps have taken over the city. Lisbon has gone to the dogs! One of them screamed. This imagined scene put a smile on Vincent's face.

Fryda thought of other things, like her bonsai trees and her time in Japan before she became a widow. Her fate a bit luckier than most.

If I can just get my hands on a bonsai tree, Fryda said, my luck might change.

A bonsai tree?

Yes. Do you know what a bonsai tree looks like?

No.

They are not one of these trees you see around you. They are small like a plotted plant. I had many in my garden in Japan.

Japan? Vincent was taken aback.

Everyone needs a companion, Fryda said. How can one go in life without another? Without someone or something to love? How is that possible?

Vincent turned his head and couldn't muster a response. He just looked at this woman with the green toenails who spoke of bonsai trees and needing a companion.

The bouts of silence between them was a welcome relief. Vincent noticed that he was content to be seated next to this matriarch of the homeless. Off in the distance, he faintly heard what sounded like a lute. And amid the aimless wanderings of most people, they were approached by a young woman from the church across the street for a donation. She held out a small silver bucket with a handle.

Doacao para os pobres, por favor?

This young girl must be clueless, Vincent thought.

She still stood there, arm outstretched, hoping for a

coin or bill to be dropped into the bucket. Vincent bent forward to peek into the pail and saw only a handful of coins. He wondered if this was a scam, the young girl collecting for herself.

He looked over at Fryda who smiled at the girl of middle school age. Nothing about this youngster gave any impression if she came from poverty. She had a very expressive face with big eyes and large eyebrows. Her stringy hair blew in the wind, her eyes sparked with anticipation.

Vincent shook his head to decline. Fryda then pulled out a small pouch that hung from her neck and pinched out a coin. She dropped in in the bucket. The young girl smiled. Her eyes grew absurdly large. Fryda continued to smile, her gaze like a mother looking at her child.

You're sweet to do this, Fryda said. *Boa sorte.*

For the next half hour, Fryda and Vincent spoke of various things. It was obvious this was not the same person who was once sought for her counsel and wisdom. No longer did she have a group of tramps clinging to her every word. It seemed as if Gertrude was the catalyst and with her death, gone went Fryda's popularity.

She finally said after another bout of silence that it was time for her to read. Fryda took out a magnifying glass and pulled a book from one of the plastic bags in her cart. She then began to read, hunched over like a mollusk, shutting out everything, even Vincent.

Later, as Vincent exited the park in a trance since he consumed a couple of Percocets—he saw the young girl from earlier eating an ice cream with a friend with her earnings. She didn't notice Vincent. She also didn't see Fausto who stood in the pond staring at the ducks with an empty Coke bottle in his hand. Vincent saw his friend thru the milky haze of the morphine kick. He inhaled the painless bliss of addiction. And no matter what anyone else in the park said, thought or believed—there stood Fausto knee-deep in one of the ponds.

PANTS DOWN +
TURNING TRICKS + WE ALL SIN

Kiki was caught with her pants down, literally, in the showers of the rectory. After being discarded by the grocer, Andrea began turning *tricks* in the stalls, along with another female friend. Needing money or other favors she would hold these trysts right below the nose of Father Gabrielo. She brought men in from the outside under the guise of being homeless. It seemed like a great deal of intricate scheming. But there was a window of time during dinner when there was enough confusion and when the younger priests, those who helped serve food, were distracted or not trained to be vigilant.

Kiki knew of a door that lead to a series of hallways which led to the showers. The door was on the south side of church where deliveries were made. This door was often unused, always left open, no need to bolt or lock it. Vincent knew of it. It was a somewhat magical exit since it revealed a fantastic view of the Alfama and the river.

Gabrielo further shamed the two women on their walk of shame as they strode by their peers on their final exit from the church. Escorted in handcuffs, he spouted some nonsensical proverbs at them—*You can't have your cake and eat it too. You've made your bed, now you're going to lie in it,* etcetera. The police nodded their heads in blank agreement and the vagrants mocked him when his back was turned.

Andrea exited with swagger, her hubris on full display, her chest swollen out. Knowing her sexual appetite had carried her this far, why should she abandon what she enjoyed? Her excess was to dwell in excess.

I love cock!

Those were her exact words. She yelled it as she passed. Several times. Fausto always bragged that his one-time girl was a nympho and not to be confused with nymph. She definitely was not a magical sprite sprinkling fairy dust. Her bounty was in flesh.

You do what you have to do.

Truer words were not spoken as Vincent reminded himself after this latest drama. Raw sex—given and received. It is what it is. Everything comes after. Most don't want to admit it. Kiki sinned. So what? We all sin.

APRICOTS +
GRAND WIZARD + BLOOD GUSHES

Vincent arrived at Martim Moniz to talk to the grocer. He had to find out about Fausto and bring closure to what really happened to his friend. His previous night's dream had Fausto urging him to kiss this particular Asian woman. Every time he leaned in to kiss the woman on the lips, she turned her head at the last second to give Vincent her cheek instead. Every single time it truly felt that he would get to kiss her lips but it was not to be. This made Fausto roar with laughter as he was wedged in between the two and doing this play-by-play as if he were at a sporting event. Come on! Get closer! Make a move! Stop being such a pussy!

Vincent peered into the grocer's store, wanted to make certain the coast was clear. He didn't want to draw too much attention. He needed a couple of minutes to ask what he needed to ask, get the response he hoped for and move on. The grocer was a large man, almost double Fausto's size. Hairy. Sported a gnarly, wieldy beard that was in fashion.

He was at the counter counting to himself, possibly

taking stock or adding the profits from the week. Vincent double-checked the surroundings before he approached him. He looked both ways as if he were crossing a street.

Com licenca?

Yes? The grocer didn't look up from his paperwork.

Pardon?

He glanced up and it took him a fraction of a second to realize that Vincent was not the type he wanted in his store.

What do you want?

I have a question...

What? A pause. Come on, spit it out.

I want to ask about a friend of mine.

Friend?

Yes, his name was—

A female voice was heard from the back of the store.

The grocer shouted, *Que?!*

O que come os damascos. She said something about apricots from what Vincent gathered.

I don't care! The grocer screamed back.

Don't blame me! Was her response.

Make sure you bring them out! Don't leave them back there!

Silence.

Did you hear me! The grocer shouted some more.

More silence.

The woman stepped into the store from the back entrance. Hands on her hips, apron smeared with God knows what, her hair frazzled and knotty.

Voce vai ajudar? She asked with one eyed raised.

The giant mumbled to himself hating every bit of his marriage by the looks of it.

Eh? Say it again. Hire someone for this shit. I'm not breaking my back.

How many times—if I go back there and you're playing cards—

You come do it. You do it! She was now gesturing with one hand in the same motion, slicing the air upwards.

Don't. Don't. Don't. The giant repeated.

She exited, still slicing at the air.

The grocer grumbled, besides himself. The words Vincent made out were *stupid woman.* He looked up and still saw Vincent in his store. The giant was losing patience.

Get out. Come on, get the fuck out.

Do you know Fausto. He was a friend. You knew him.

Que? Que? The grocer set down his checklist and came out from behind the counter.

He's been missing. I thought you might know—

Que?! By now he had stepped out and was ready to lay hands on Vincent or something worse.

Please, he's a friend. I know you know him. He told me.

The grocer stopped in his tracks. Vincent's remarks shocked him into inaction. He stood frozen like some overgrown grand wizard.

Please, I know you can help. Tell me something, Vincent pleaded.

Of course the grocer knew of whom he was speaking. Embarrassed into rage, thinking that this lowlife in front of him was the beneficiary of sordid gossip, his reputation and livelihood could not be tarnished.

What happened next was inevitable. He struck Vincent upside his head. More like a slap with a cupped hand.

Vincent stumbled backward, his arms flailed in a balletic way, helping him stay upright. With another lunge, the giant struck Vincent on one side of his head and then the opposite. Bam bam! in quick succession. This time Vincent flew to the floor and skidded to a stop, such was the brute's strength.

The grocer grabbed a broom and whacked Vincent on the back. Vincent tried to rise but each blow kept him on all fours. Whack! Whack! And with every strike the grocer screamed—Get out! Get out! By this time, his wife now re-entered and was beyond words—which was a first. The blunt force of each strike kept Vincent in the same spot. By this time, with sheer impulse, he rolled in a different direction which gave him enough time to at least rise to his knees.

Sure enough, the grocer lumbered in pursuit, one step of his covered a lot of ground. He struck the beleaguered Vincent on the shoulder, broke the broomstick in two. This pissed the giant off even further. He screamed, *Merda! Merda!* Under siege, Vincent grasped at the air. His wife screamed as well. A melee of grunts, thuds, screams and with Vincent's hair now being pulled, it turned into a scrum with both violent and comic potential.

Again, because of sheer impulse, Vincent wildly swung his arm and caught the giant's knee with his elbow. This brought the behemoth to crash down atop him. Both men then rolled in opposite directions and Vincent ended up next to one half of the broomstick. He grabbed it and lunged at the grocer. He then took the stick and brought it over the grocer's head and pressed it against the large man's neck. By this time, a few passersby were not only intrigued but peeked into the darkness of the store to gather what all the commotion was about.

The grocer's wife screamed, Help! Madman! She ran in circles as the grocer was again atop Vincent but was being choked this time round. Vincent pressed the stick against the man's windpipe. Grunting, spitting, kicking both his feet — the giant gasped for air. Vincent was being crushed by the man's weight. The grocer turned over and rolled a few times until he crashed Vincent into the counter. This dislodged him from the broomstick. He then leapt up and kicked the giant in his ribcage while his wife hit him wildly, screaming.

Before anything else took place and onlookers could get any further details into their heads, Vincent slipped out of the store, turned the corner and made his way quickly down Rua da Mourari where he headed east, blood gushing from his nose.

PSALM 23

Many didn't survive the trip from Warsaw. At least a quarter of the hundreds packed like cattle in the train transport. They were told they were being relocated to a labor camp in the Ukraine. The cold did not discriminate. Collectively, they tried to survive—body heat, makeshift fires, the straw and newspaper they stuffed inside their clothing. Most times, it didn't matter. Starvation, frostbite, hypothermia, no food or water, suffocation, delay after delay.

It was the winter of 1942. The prisoners could see through the slits of the boxcar walls at the passing Polish landscape. Some knew they were heading north being familiar with the railway system and the terrain. They were not heading east as the Germans promised. Field after field with always a thin layer of frost. Tree after leafless tree, grazing livestock, on and on, most huddled against the cold or inhabiting some solitary space in all this bleak vastness.

Where are we headed?

Some knew of their fate. Others believed of what they heard as pure gossip, rumors, nothing could be further from the truth. It was beyond human capacity—mass killings? Extermination? And still the train lurched on, destination unknown. Equal amounts of desperation and excrement. At least some families were fortunate enough to not be separated as of yet. Herded from the deportation site—in this case the Warsaw ghetto.

Eventually the train swung a bit eastward and it was at this moment if you turned your head, you noticed the person next to you was no longer breathing. They could not fall to the boxcar floor because there was no room to do so. They died upright. The numbers of the dead climbed with the number of delays and the length of the journey. All other trains took precedence and it was not uncommon to stay immobile for hours. Children and infants were famished. Mothers of newborns were crazed, inconsolable.

The train eventually arrived at Treblinka as most did from Warsaw. As the boxcar doors opened, German SS and Ukrainian kapos barked instructions at the dazed and frozen prisoners. The selection process began immediately. To the right was slave labor. To the left were the gas chambers. The elderly, women and children were torn from the healthy and able-bodied, already selected to perish within the hour. The cold was unceasing. The gusts of wind didn't help. Ninety percent who made the trip were in line to make the quarter mile trudge beneath the entrance to the camp—*Death Gate*.

Within all this tumult—freezing gusts of wind, constant beatings, barking dogs—most eyes were glued downward at the layer of frost crunching beneath their feet. However, miracle of miracles, there was the promise of a hot shower. Anything to get warm! Anything!!

And when the chance arose they would peek at their

surroundings, at this most alien of places. Two tracks, one arriving, the other departing and no sign of civilization for miles. Only these nondescript brick buildings and the strange smell, a mix of cyanide and the stench of some mass crematorium. With each step, there was a gnawing suspicion—something did not add up. But hot showers were promised. Warmth!

They stripped naked. Hair was shorn. Infants wailed. Children shivered uncontrollably. All little ones clung to their mothers' breasts. The elderly could barely stand. Their knees buckled. Some sensed death beyond the large iron doors. Women began to scream. A German pastor tried to calmed them as they filed in, told them to recite passages, reassure themselves. It's okay, move forward, as many as possible. Warm showers! *Gehen! Hab keine Angst!* Go! Don't be afraid!

An entire mass of bodies was being crammed into an underground passage. Some seemed resigned to meet their maker. Ibrahim's father began reciting a passage from Psalms—*The Lord is my shepherd. I shall not want. He causes me to lie down in green pastures. He leads me besides still waters. He restores my soul.* The iron doors clanged behind them. A mass of writhing bodies, jockeyed for an inch of space. *He leads me in paths of righteousness for His name's sake. Even when I walk in the valley of darkness, I will fear no evil for You are with me: Your rod and Your staff-they comfort me.* All went black. More screams. There was not a sliver of space. Children suffocated. Bedlam. In one flash, warm water began to fall from the spouts above. Relief, warmth, beatitude. *You set a table before me in the presence of my adversaries; You anointed my head with oil; my cup overflows.* And then the cyanide caplets dispersed. The poison acted quickly. Choking black, eyes bulged, pain crawled out of pores. Mothers and fathers did what they had to do to spare their children from suffering, killed them with their own hands. *May only goodness and kindness pursue me all the days of my life and I will in the house of the Lord for length of days.* This lasted another thirty minutes. Then silence. Vapor. The last groans dying out.

Ibrahim recites this Psalm every night before sleep takes him.

GOLDEN SHOWER + FUCK YOUR MOTHER + NO MORE CHURCH

Vincent woke to a warm, yellow trickle splash atop his head. As he came to, he looked up to see an enormous, bushy vagina straddle his face and another stream of urine slashing down on him. After some commotion and some banter and laughter, he realized that a woman was in fact straddled above his face, pissing on him. The smell of urine was now evident. It drenched his hair and made its way down the back of his neck. The woman, along with a band of other homeless laughed, pointed, mocked as they sauntered away.

Besides himself, Vincent gave chase. Two men from the group, much larger than Vincent, knocked him over, gave him a couple of kicks to the groin and kicked dirt on him. The ridicule now complete, they walked away as if nothing happened. Vagrants exercised their own levels of hierarchy and subjugation.

FODA SUA MAE!! Vincent screamed.

They disappeared from view. He walked to the nearest fountain and rinsed up. He removed the top half of what he wore, washed and wrung it out. Waiting for his shirt to dry, his back on the balustrade, his face up to the sun, he recalled the previous night. Gabrielo was outside the church talking to a group of police officers. A small congregation of younger priests were doing their best to calm the rest of the community that gathered, including other vagrants who assumed another victim was found. Vincent saw that Gabrielo was visibly anxious and upset. The younger priests did their best not to feed into his manic energy. This was his pulpit and from the bits of what Vincent could hear—Martim Moniz / grocery store/ wife—he knew his time was over at the church.

Vincent thought of his belongings, the handful of books he possessed, his clothing, his talcum powder and the pinch of weed he hid in the lining of his suitcase. The sunlight combated how low Vincent felt—bruised, humiliated, the hot flashes. His entire torso was the color of alabaster and the rings around his eyes were tinged yellow. He was feeling the sting of never seeing his belongings again, his lack of a home, his nowhere identity. This was absolute. he could never return back to Santa Lucia.

He opened his eyes fearful of what he would see. He saw two birds zip from left to right. East to west. Vincent's eyes followed them beyond the hazy fringe of sunlight. The birds flew rapidly, with purpose, past a thicket of trees and from view. Vincent put his chin to his chest and closed his eyes again. Life went on, barely.

DAYS NUMBERED + ONIONS
AND MOLD + CROSS THEY BEAR

Time was against Ibrahim. His days were numbered. He sensed he would not last much longer. He recalled an elderly woman from his synagogue a few years back standing up during service and thanked all those present for the last fifty years of her time at the church. She said that this would be the last time she would see all of them. And sure enough, she died peacefully a couple of days later, in her sleep. She knew it. Simple as that.

He hadn't seen Vincent for a couple of days. He lost track of him, the first time he had done so since he arrived in Lisbon. Vincent's movements became more erratic but the one thing Ibrahim counted on was his return to the church.

The little man chewed on his fingernails, a habit he was prone to. Years of planning, research, sifting through hundreds of documents, the dead ends, the hopeful leads, the large sum of money he spent on his quest for revenge— led him to Lisbon—to this moment.

Was Vincent the right man? He was no doubt conflicted. Was this vagrant the son of the man who had a hand in the murder of his family at Treblinka? This delusional amnesiac? Ibrahim convinced himself that he was not a madman. Those who committed the atrocities were the madmen. They were a stain on humanity. He needed to rid the stain. But was Vincent the One?

He arrived at Santa Lucia to speak with Gabrielo. Ibrahim noted how airless his office was. He sat there with his leather case resting on his lap and his hands face down on the case, looking at the man with the stern, bushy eyebrows. Both men sat there in silence. The place smelled of a strange mix of onions and mold.

Gabrielo broke the quiet. I have no information to give you. I have no idea of his whereabouts, neither do the authorities.

I appreciate your meeting with me, Father, I'm sure you are a busy man.

Gabriel waved off any inconvenience. Another beautiful day in Lisbon, is it not?

Why don't you crack open a window? Ibrahim thought to himself. Yes, the weather has been fantastic.

Are you enjoying Lisbon? Are you here for business or vacationing?

Well, a mix of both. That is why I am here in front of you.

Tell me...

I seek the man who assaulted the grocer. I have information that might help the police in this matter.

Namely?

Do you not know his history? Do you know why he's in Lisbon?

I know some but not enough to satisfy your curiosity.

Is there anything you can tell me or anywhere I can

find him? This is a matter of utmost importance. So many years of—

I'm sorry but you must know that he is a vagrant. He had been fortunate enough to find shelter and food here. Yes, he worked for it but many of them suffer from mental illness or some form of mental incapacity.

Yes, I understand. But—

This vagramt assaulted an upstanding member of the community. What else is there to say? The man's wife is in a state of shock. Never in her thirty years of running that store did she experience such a thing!

All well and good, all well and good—Ibrahim's hands were now up in the air gesturing compliance—but supposedly this man has no past. From what I know, he is an amnesiac.

Most of them are! Gabrielo let out a burst of laughter. This does not change anything.

Father, the man has a medical condition.

Another laugh. Most of them are delusional. Half of them suffer from hallucinations!

Another bout of silence. Ibrahim's attention turned again to the smell in the room. Beads of sweat collected on his brow. The priest's office suddenly became oppressive. Usually a man of little movement Ibrahim fidgeted a great deal.

They talk of ghosts, pirates, dragons-they play act! I see them. I walk amongst them, Gabrielo continued.

Are you implying that—

Most of them cannot assimilate into normal society. Try having a normal conversation with them. They are migrants. They have no home. That is the cross they bear.

But the man we are speaking of made his home at the

church for an entire year. Maybe more.

Greater numbers of people lead to greater misery. This is what we are seeing.

His name is Vincent, Ibrahim pressed.

His name? What is a name to these homeless? This country is suffering from a CRISIS! Things are not well. There are bigger concerns. I have nothing to give you. Gabrielo smiled, stood up, extended a hand. There are agencies that deal with these matters. My apologies for letting you down.

Ibrahim's back and buttock were soaked in sweat. He sat for a couple of moments, grossly uncomfortable, uncertain to continue or not. His body was failing him, his right knee buckled as he stood. He held the ledge of the chair to steady himself.

Gabrielo made no effort to help the little man. I can get one of my assistants to show you out. Ibrahim reached into his attache case and pulled out a card with his information.

Please call me, if you hear anything or if you can help me in any way.

Reading the card—Mr. Mintz—may God be with you.

GOSSAMER VEIL +
CRUSADE + LEAVE IT ALONE

Sleepless for the past two evenings, Ibrahim lost track of Vincent. His eyes betrayed him for the past twenty-four hours. Lack of sleep draped a gossamer veil over Lisbon's streets and metro stations. He surveyed the metro stops with a watchful eye. Cais do Sodre, Rossio, Barreiro. The strain on his eyes—hundreds of passengers, tourists, locals, those traveling from south to north or vice versa—ground him to a fine dust by the end of each day. And still, he couldn't sleep.

How could I let him slip away! What a fool! I am stupid and weak!

The one constant was his grip on his attache case. The rest of him wilted. His heart grew weaker, his breathing grew shorter. Whatever wound him up, the quest to finish what he set out to do, now threatened to collapse.

He missed home. Israel. His path was ordained. Ibrahim did not consider himself a murderer. Yes, he poisoned those that poisoned his own family. He made sure they suffered, which they did, much like his loved ones. This has always been his very own redress. This was his path to make good. Revenge seemed too trivial a concept. This was beyond hate. This was to make good, set aright. It was Ibrahim's very own crusade. There was a purity in his attempt or so he firmly believed.

Instead, he wheezed heavily in Lisbon, his own end nearing with each breathe. The air coming off the Atlantic didn't agree with him. The Mediterranean breeze was kinder to the little man's lungs. What is the saying—caught between a rock and a hard place—that's how Ibrahim felt.

Regardless, he scoped and scoped. The various hundreds he did observe became a blur. His head spun, his eyes watered, his head pounded. The anxiety from his enormous mistake weakened him both in body and mind. Each passing hour made him doubt his purpose in this foreign place that he didn't like. He didn't enjoy the customs, the stupid fascination with sardines, the little tart pastries the tourists were fanatical about, the young drunks spewing obscenities—the malice in their blank stares.

It was times like this in which he hated himself for taking on this quest. And he doubted more and more that this Vincent was the son of the man who was the catalyst of his family's death. This vagrant who didn't seem to have any idea of who, what or why he was in Lisbon. Why go after this person? This nobody? Leave it alone, go home, die quietly.

BARBED WIRE +
LETTER Z + LAUGHING CHILDREN

Vincent had no idea what day or month it was. His body and mind became tainted. He kept pursuing Fausto, believing him to be in Lisbon. Maybe it was the last opportunity for him to believe in something, the possibility of salvaging a friendship. Vincent didn't take it lightly nor did his body and febrile imagination. *Acredito. Acredito.* He kept saying to himself.

But what necessarily did he believe? That Fausto was alive, here in Lisbon and he would prove it? We are friends. I will save this friendship.

But what hypocrisy! Vincent couldn't see it, too blinded by the Lisbon that no longer belonged to him and his misguided attempts to find his fat friend. This Lisbon spat him out, no longer cared for his kind. His existence had become a victim of his own abstractions.

Dogs barked at him. *Cale se!! Cale se!!* He screamed in the black of night, up and down the hilly streets.

The stiff smell of salt water was pungent. He must've been near the river. Vincent closed his eyes, took in a full breath and for a brief second, he felt that he was on a trajectory over the Atlantic, lifting higher and higher. That distinct smell took him elsewhere, where all he noticed was an expanse of sea. He imagined himself a seabird, scaling higher and higher. The height and sense of freedom, the further up he soared, and with it, his own body became lighter.

More barking snapped him out of his reverie. And with it, the pain resumed, the heat of his body rose, his sanity crept closer to something he didn't want to pursue. He found himself snagged on barbed wire. Where am I? He looked around, the barking still present but now in the far distance.

What neighborhood is this?

Everywhere he looked, barbed wire lined every stone wall or was coiled tightly between buildings. Very strange, he thought. Along the horizon, set against the background light, the thorny rope of more barbed wire could be seen. This was more like a prison than a city neighborhood, Vincent thought.

What the hell is this?

A man was seen, his slumped walk and smallish figure in contrast to the buildings and long shadows. He came up a curved walkway which lead directly to Vincent. He wheezed heavily. Vincent thought it was Ibrahim who walked toward him. The old man's cap veiled half his face. The other half was haggard and pitted by age. Now at arm's length away, Vincent noticed that it wasn't Ibrahim—the little man that made him very uneasy. Regardless, this stranger stood in front of Vincent, not in a threatening way but with his eyes cast downward.

He took off his cap and extended it toward Vincent. He just stood there, his drooping eyes still directed at

Vincent's feet. He eventually spoke, saying only one word. Vincent didn't answer. The old buzzard asked again, his extended arm now shaking. Vincent told him he didn't understand the language. The man uttered it again. Then again. It seemed like he was asking for money. Vincent gestured that he didn't have any, nearly screamed at the old man to take a good look at him.

Do I look like I have money!! He wanted to scream.

This exchange triggered another hot flash in Vincent. He pulled out his pockets, tried to communicate any way he knew how. Nothing helped. The man kept uttering the same word. It sounded like he spoke in Hebrew. No matter, Vincent's discomfort kept climbing. He slammed the hat out of the man's head and shoved him against the stone wall.

The barking ceased entirely as the old man was upheld by the wall, half slumped over, still avoided eye contact with Vincent. Half of Vincent wanted to continue beating on the poor stranger. His other half put a stop to this deranged impulse.

Silence.

The old man's chest heaved in and out. I'm sorry, Vincent finally muttered. Sorry, again and even quieter than the first. He extended his hand. The stranger didn't take it. Vincent felt remorse. He thought how could he assault this brittle, bow-legged man who could hardly stand? He must have been close to eighty or even older. What was he asking? Why was he here? Where the hell am I? What is this neighborhood?

The old buzzard began to undo the top two buttons of his shirt. His fingers shook. It took a couple of moments for Vincent to realize what was happening. He whispered—

What are you doing?

The old man continued. Vincent stepped back, almost tumbled on one of the stone steps. Vincent urged him to stop. *Do you understand?* Before he could say another word, the stranger pulled down the left side of his shirt. Still leaning against the wall, he now looked directly at Vincent, the area above his heart now exposed.

Vincent was shocked to see how skeletal the man was. He then noticed a series of numbers tattooed above the stranger's heart followed by the letter Z. It struck Vincent that the old man was gaunt like the figures in his recent dreams. *Why is he doing this? Why is he showing me this?* Vincent shook his head at the man, not understanding his intentions. I don't have any money. I don't have anything. I don't know what you want? What do you want! Vincent kept blathering, hoped something would make sense during this encounter.

The stranger pointed to the Z on his chest. He began to say something—a string of words. The more he spoke, the more it did sound like he spoke Hebrew. Again, nothing was understood. The man became more animated, if you can call it that. Still peeled to the wall, his finger on the letter shook violently. The barking dogs kicked up again. The old man didn't let up, his words now unfurled out of his mouth. Vincent felt as if he were roasting in an oven, believed his hair was aflame. He closed his eyes, put his fist in his mouth to muffle a scream.

Silence.

Vincent opened his eyes. More silence. The old man cut a hazy figure—half man, half apparition. His chest no longer exposed, he pushed himself off the wall. He took a deep breath, drew in Lisbon's briny air. Both men heard a group of children off in the distance laughing. What a strange hour for children to be out, Vincent thought. The old man gave one final look at Vincent. The look signified something particular, some secret that would become unearthed at some later date as if the truth could not be exposed here at this moment.

The old man went off into the night. Vincent stood there as confused and perplexed as an infant out of the womb.

NUMBER 28 + SUICIDE + I'M SORRY

Vincent and Ibrahim crisscrossed Lisbon from one end to the other. This went on for a few days. Their fortunes didn't change, only their desire to continue on in Lisbon for their own obsessive reasons. The church closed its doors as a shelter for the poor. More homeless were thrust out into the streets. Most doors were being closed on the poor. The streets teemed with vagrants, most of them asked themselves—

Where to go? How to survive?

There were a couple of occasions when Ibrahim almost hit the mark. Once, at Praca Luis de Camoes and the other at Jardim da Estrela. Ibrahim was riding the Number 28 tram, Lisbon's most popular, as it passed Vincent's favorite park. Packed with tourists, the little man was draped out of the tram, his right arm dangling. The man from Israel got caught up in the sight and sounds of Old Lisbon. He let his guard down, the constant surveillance wore him down, his heart grew weaker, both literally and figuratively. So he absently gazed at the old ladies, the younger children, the couples in love and felt he could touch them on their shoulders or pat them on the heads, feeling so close as the tram skimmed by, hugging the corners of Alfama's old buildings and churches.

The tram stopped at Basilica Estrela where a slew of Chinese tourists boarded, along with a great deal of noise and bustle. A large woman—a local—since she muttered in Portuguese of how sick she was of tourists as she shoved her way to a seat next to Ibrahim. Her large frame forced the little man further out the window, his head and upper half of his body now hung outside the tram. Disgusted by this forced contact, he turned his face toward the Basilica. If he happened to look to his left, past the wall of tourists, he would've spotted Vincent near the entrance to the park, just standing there — his image a shell of his former self. Parents scrambled to grab their children's arms when they noticed the haggard, near-deranged vagrant muttering nonsense to himself.

Ibrahim muttered under his own breath as the elephantine woman refreshed her makeup, her right elbow kneading into him. Not being able to locate Vincent tore the little Jew apart. Unable to sleep, he begged his father's forgiveness and in his quiet moments, past the stifled sobs, he thought of his mother and siblings. His heart grew weaker, his appetite for death grew stronger. For the first time, he thought of suicide. He thought of taking the poison he administered to others.

Ibrahim's thoughts overwhelmed him, so much so that he was not really seeing anything, not looking at anywhere in particular. How could I be so weak? How could I be so stupid? Followed by—I'm sorry, I'm sorry, I'm sorry...

Both men practiced an aimless wandering. They breathed indecision. Fausto kept appearing around every corner and just as quickly dissolved like the early morning fog that camped on the banks of the Tagus. Ibrahim's self-pity and misery bulldozed any logic. Too stricken by this inexcusable mistake (which he thought impossible), he began to lose his sensibilities. His reasoning went the way of Vincent's. Both of them cursed their misfortune and at times wished themselves dead.

WE ACCEPT ALL

I have a child. Had. I had a child. I miss my little girl. I recall how excited she would get when we would go fishing along the Seine. Summer days, early in the morning. She loved getting up on Saturday mornings, shaking me awake, telling her that I needed my espresso before we could do anything. She rolled her eyes every time I said it. The stories she would tell me as we sat and fished. Hardly ever caught anything and if we did, we would cut it loose and throw it back. The thrill in her eyes every time we did so. How sad she felt when we had trouble with the hook one time and the fish just laid there in her palms. Her telling me to hurry up. The excitement in her voice. How it trembled. A sign of her age.

Those are the memories I recall. Our feet dangled over the stony banks. The river and the small boats gliding by. My daughter waved at them, shouting—*bonne journee!* And always, I would remind her that she would scare the fish. Sometimes, she would go on and on, talking about school, her friends at school, the teachers she disliked, her favorite foods, the latest trends, how she always wanted to learn how to knit so she could knit me a sweater for a

Christmas present and then begging me to take her to the butterfly garden at the Jardin des Papillons.

Have you ever been there? It's an experience. A thrilling one. But at the same time so calming. Isn't that interesting—both thrilling and calming. It gave my daughter such a rush. Truth be told, it was the same for me. Everything slowed. Car horns, the whine from those damn scooters, the ambulance sirens—didn't exist. Another ten minutes! She would beg. Another fifteen! I couldn't refuse her. You were enchanted, enthralled. You felt safe inside that place as if you were lying on white sand staring at clouds all night long.

This was the most Andres spoke to Vincent. Vincent sat there and quietly acknowledged this by giving his friend an appreciative glance as Andres looked off into the far horizon knowing that is where he belonged— somewhere beyond. Vincent possibly felt the same as his fingers tingled as he moved them. An unusual feeling welled up in Vincent's heart, signifying that this would be the last time Andres would pay a visit—their last quiet moment—until another time. Vincent didn't want to look up knowing what he would find.

Vincent breathed quietly to himself. Inhaled cool air that actually soothed him, scraped some of the edge away. His eyes still aimed at his fingers, he tried to recall the younger priest's name but couldn't. It was there on the tip of his tongue and as Vincent kept scanning his fingers, from pinky to thumb, the name still evaded him.

He reached out a hand to his friend but there was no Andres. Vincent then looked up and scanned the sky from east to west, north to south, and hoped by looking at the stars there would be the providence or counsel he desperately sought. This evaded him as well. Still gazing at the vault of sky, the last words from Gabrielo's sermon resurfaced in his mind—

We are a peace-loving people, us Portuguese. We are a simple people. We accept all. Look at those who sit next to you. Turn to them. We accept all. These are not false words. There are no false prophets here, in this church.

We accept ALL.

I will share with you a passage from Psalms. *Blessed are those who do not walk in step with the wicked or stand in the way that sinners take or sit in the company of mockers.* We have our troubles. These are solemn times. Something unnameable has gripped us. Who among us is a survivor? Yes, a crisis has hit our country. We now find ourselves victims of unruly circumstance. Right outside our very own church we have those who murder, rape, molest. Right on our very own steps! How can we stay righteous? Behave righteously? This is an—

AFFLICTION.

So, I ask you again—who among us is a survivor?

PENANCE + FLEA
MARKET + GOD'S VENGEANCE

The little man sat with his hands on his knees, his body hunched over, sucking in air through his large nostrils. Death was close. He sensed it. Ibrahim mistakenly thought the air in Israel could cure him but it wouldn't matter. His costly error—the one he would never forgive himself for—quickened death's grip. He let his father down. He let his entire family down. His lungs were collapsing. This was his penance.

Vincent walked among the throng of people at Feira da Ladra, the flea market near the church. Back in his old neighborhood, he half-noticed his fellow homeless but none he completely recognized. He felt like an ass—restless, ragged, indifferent. Some youngsters went by, mocked him, laughed until he was out of earshot. Vincent heard someone repeat Tuesday! Tuesday! Tuesday! Not understanding the reference (the flea market being open on both Tuesdays and Saturdays). Annoyed, he mumbled it out loud, Tuesdays! Tuesdays! Tuesdays!

Eventually, Vincent headed west on Rua de San Vincente. Large crowds bothered him. He was glad to be rid of the flea market. He crossed R. Sao Tome. What he failed to notice was Ibrahim who spotted him, miracu- lously, at the flea market and gave chase. The little man shuffled quickly, wheezed greatly.

Crossing R. Sao Tome, Ibrahim almost toppled over. He willed himself forward. This was his opportunity. Vincent climbed many steps, not slowing any, in the direction of the church. Ibrahim's upward climb—possibly a pursuit to his death—as Vincent's speed and youth were difficult to overcome. The old man's lungs burned, his lower back tensed up, spasms contorted his face.

Vincent cleared the last step into Jardim de Castilho, now roped off due to the recent murders. Nothing in particular prompted this frantic climb under the noonday sun. He felt compelled to do it—a force of unknown origin dictated it.

He noticed the blue tiles that depicted the Christian victory over the Moors on the side of the church. On closer view, he saw the swords of the Crusaders drip with blood and the Moors lain slaughtered at their feet—many at the very spot Vincent now stood. A plague ravaged the city after the long battle. Some say it was God's vengeance on the Christians and their barbaric ways.

It was eerily quiet and not one soul could be seen in the popular tourist spot. Vincent turned his head toward the garden pool and as he did so a flash of steel glinted in the sun. Before he could react, Tristao's knife plunged into Vincent's side in three quick thrusts—pff, pff, pff. As the final stab wrenched deeper near Vincent's lungs, Tristao clenched both his grip and his teeth and hissed—

I always keep my promises, asshole.

He then shoved Vincent off his blade and the vagrant

stumbled and fell into the shallow pool. As Tristao fled, Ibrahim arrived, weary in body and spirit. This is it, the little man thought. His body tensed and he collapsed on the last slab of steps. His face was stuck on the cement. There was a gash in his forehead. Blood poured freely. He was concussed as his chest heaved. The hot cement warmed him. It felt good as nothing else did. His head felt as if a pile of bricks struck him. Dazed, almost numb, he could not feel his fingertips.

Ibrahim inhaled slowly, the warmth of the cement filled his lungs and his exhale—a slow, protracted one—released half the life left in his body. With that, a slew of memories rushed at him. Faces he knew and loved, his street, his bookshelves, the music of Bach, the knish he ate every Sunday evening, the latkes his mother would make, his father's intense gaze as he played chess, the smell of rosewater on his sister's cheeks, the life draining from his parents' faces as they read the Nazi order to relocate into the ghetto.

Halfway between life and death, his face still smeared on concrete, Ibrahim saw the vagrant's arm slung over the lip of the pool. The sun was strong, his eyes blinked, everything began to blur.

And before his final breath, he heard his dad's last gurgling breath in the gas chamber at Treblinka. He heard fingernails scratch against the wall. He barely heard his mother's last whimper. Just as he barely saw the smudge that was the pool of blood Vincent floated in.

All went black.

AND THEN THE SEALS

When Vincent opened his eyes, he saw a rectangular shaped skylight. Framed in the window was the blue sky. It took him a bit of time to realize what he looked at. For a brief moment, he thought he was dead. He felt no pain, his mind was completely uncluttered, his eyes looked on a world as transparent as ever.

As he came to, he noticed that he sat propped up on a hospital bed. He had the room to himself. From the soft yellow of the walls to the creme-colored bedding to the blue sky above, everything seemed vivid and alive. Resisting the temptation to close his eyes, he turned to see an IV pole and his reflection in the steel basin next to him. He noticed the heavy bandage wrapped around his torso.

Baffled, he took a moment to sink back into the pillow and looked up into the aquamarine blue. He sat, still and contemplative. He began to remember—he was stabbed, he lost a good deal of blood, he was lucky to be alive, the blade was small, missed his lungs by a fraction of an inch. The doctor told him the police would come by when he was less confused. Ironically, he didn't feel confused, only heavily sedated. Vincent's thoughts were clear.

His eyelids fluttered. The image of Tristao came to him. A flash of hate as he thrust the knife in his side. The devil in disguise. Vincent relived it as it played out like a film montage and his heart rate increased with it.

He felt as light as a feather. The heart monitor proved that he possessed a heartbeat, that he was alive and breathing. The blue of the framed sky in the skylight also added to the feeling that he was in the transitive place between life and death. He sunk deeper into his pillow, his eyes grew weary, he felt good and at peace. Eventually, the sunlight warmed him and he began to pass into a lucid sleep.

He imagined himself in blue water, similar to the blue framed by the skylight. And swimming next to him was Fausto. Both men actually suspended right below the surface, breathing easily, arms treading back and forth. Vincent noticed Fausto's swim trunks were a bit too tight and hiked up his butt crack. This made him laugh. The seals arrived. And like underwater gazelles they captivated both men, who grinned from ear to ear. Vincent laughed at his friend, the seals were playful and mischievous, Fausto was doing underwater flips.

And as Vincent sunk deeper into sleep, his magical gift of hearing opened up to him again. Anything seemed possible as he could hear Ignacio Silva's ringing alarm clock, for he was the bank manager of Intesa San Paolo in Trieste. Silva's feet shuffled on his newly varnished wooden floors as he made his morning cup of espresso and then showered and decided to break in his new pair of shoes on this morning. He had a habit of looking at his Blackberry as he walked the ten minutes to his bank, responding to messages and emails. The loud clack of his shoes went unnoticed by his own ears. However, his employees and those who worked close to him took notice as his clacking shoes signaled his arrival—punctual as always.

His next order of business was to reply to the five requests to procure certain documents from strongbox no. 51. Only Silva or his assistant manager had access to this particular strongbox. Silva discarded four requests except for the recent one from a legal firm in Lisbon (in tandem with a police investigation), attempting to gain access to the contents inside the box. (The other four requests were from a man named I. Mintz who had previous unsolicited requests). After several phone calls Silva was faxed the proof he needed.

At times, Silva whistled as he worked. He did the same as he took the stairs down one flight past the security guard whom he passed without looking up—still whistling. All the while Vincent faded into the deepest sleep and hearing every detail—Silva's shoes, the rattling keys, the clicks his Blackberry keys made as he sent a message.

Silva made his way to the codebox and slipped his Blackberry inside his jacket pocket for no signal would reach him once inside the vault. He punched in the code, looked once again at the fax he received and pushed open the large steel door and ducked into the sealed room. He closed the door behind him, took out the fax and laid it on the table to make certain all was as it seemed. Silva took out his keys, located the smallish key with the letter T (which was the branch in Trieste) and scanned for strongbox no. 51.

Silva counted five rows from the left and one down. On his toes, he inserted the small key, pulled out the case and set it on the table. Back to his whistling, Silva propped open the front half of the case and pulled out a faded manila envelope. He laid the envelope on the table next to the case, unstrung it carefully and pulled out the contents. He placed the contents next to the now opened envelope and then proceeded to pull out a small magnifying glass from his other coat pocket. This was a necessity since some of these contents were faded and difficult to read.

There was a photograph, a stamped tin identification tag and a grayish four by six card. *Bilik—Poland, 1942* was written on the back of the photograph. When Silva turned the photograph over, he saw a group of men—most of them smiling, two with stern looks. Those at the end of both rows held clubs. The one standing in back row center was Bento Oleksandr Bilik, Vincent's father—Ukrainian by birth. Behind them were scores of Jews ready to be transported to the camps. This was the beginning stages of the Final Solution. Bilik had a hand in the shady dealings that saved lives or not. Ironically, his name meant *protector of man.*

Ibrahim's family, along with a few others, bribed him for paperwork needed to cross borders, get them to Switzerland or maybe Spain. He was paid a good deal of money. Bilik was a collaborator. Poles and Slavs did the same. Some of them did this in order to save their own skins and not meet the same fate of those in the background of the photo.

It didn't matter, Bilik took their money and still did nothing to take their names off the list. That list was everything. Sure enough, an SS raid would ensue and they would then be deported. He could have warned Ibrahim's family for he knew when the raid would happen, the day and time. He took their payment and did nothing.

Back in the hospital Vincent dreamt his improbable dream. He found himself among crashing waves. In his dream or wherever his mind was at the time, the sound of Silva's shoes was now drowned out by the sound of waves. Vincent's body tingled with salt water and wherever he happened to be, it was dusk. The clouds—the largest, most magnificent cumulus clouds—were the color of salmon pink thanks to the setting sun. And just a bit away, doing his own bit of wave-riding was Fausto. Both men came up from under as the moment allowed. They laughed and swam, dipped and dove into the waves with the grace of the same seals that Vincent loved.

Never had he felt more alive.

Now back in the air-conditioned confines of the Intesa SanPaolo Bank, Ignacio Silva placed the photograph of Vincent's father atop the manila envelope. He then took out a pair of prongs from his other jacket pocket and carefully—with a surgeon's touch—picked up the gray paper and opened up the two folded ends. Each touch of the prong left a slight indentation on the decades-old document. What he saw at the top shocked him. It was an official *Schutzstaffel*-SS stamped insignia. The red of the stamp stood out on the rather dullish gray document. The Nazis kept meticulous records during this period. It was one of the first directives with a list of Jewish family names that were to be rounded up by the young Bilik and his group and then herded onto the cattle cars for deportation to the death camp at Treblinka. The letter was dated *September 5, 1942.*

After closer inspection, bent over and looking closely through his magnifying glass, he noticed that the date was actually September 15. The number one was faded. He scanned the document from left to right and worked downward. There were fifteen family names listed. Interesting that the date and number of families coincided, Silva thought. Halfway down the list was the name MINTZ.

Next to the name written in parentheses was the word *corrompere*. It meant bribe. Right after the word was an X. Ten of the families had X's marked next to them. Silva assumed that these were the families that were chosen to be among the first wave to go to Treblinka. Another family was awarded a labor pass and another a *Schutzpass*—a letter of protection. The Mintz's were not as lucky.

Silva wouldn't know the significance of the document and why there weren't others. We will never know how Ibrahim survived or how he escaped in order to survive. It was one of those improbable stories much like the secrets and true happenings of such a time. We will never know that the young Bilik raped and impregnated Ibrahim's oldest sister who later became a victim of the war. She gave birth to Vincent's sister (many years his senior) who later met her own end by her unknown half-brother, Ibrahim.

It was all as improbable as the salmon-colored sky and emerald-blue sea in which Vincent was floating, oblivious of Fausto, whose dead and bloated body now drifted out to sea.

THE END

ABOUT ATMOSPHERE PRESS

Atmosphere Press is an independent, full-service publisher for excellent books in all genres and for all audiences. Learn more about what we do at atmospherepress.com.

We encourage you to check out some of Atmosphere's latest releases, which are available at Amazon.com and via order from your local bookstore:

Tree One, a novel by Fred Caron
Connie Undone, a novel by Kristine Brown
A Cage Called Freedom, a novel by Paul P.S. Berg
Shining in Infinity, a novel by Charles McIntyre
Buildings Without Murders, a novel by Dan Gutstein
Katastrophe: The Dramatic Actions of Kat Morgan, a young adult novel by Sylvia M. DeSantis
SEED: A Jack and Lake Creek Book, a novel by Chris S. McGee
The Testament, a novel by S. Lee Glick
Mondegreen Monk, a novel by Jonathan Kumar

ABOUT THE AUTHOR

Thomas Bazar is a novelist, poet and playwright. His plays *Momo & Toto* and *Maximus O.* were recently staged with A Band of Actors theatre collective. His poems have recently been published with Lucky Jefferson and he is at work on another novel.

CPSIA information can be obtained
at www.ICGtesting.com
Printed in the USA
FSHW020734230720
71823FS

9 781648 261084